Dungeon of Doom

"I think this foolishness has gone on long enough," said Derek. "Surrender or pay the price, Hardy!"

"I'll never surrender to you, Hannon," said Joe, backing away from Derek's outthrust sword. Out of the corner of his eye Joe could see the sword that Derek had knocked out of his hand. If only he could reach it in time.

Suddenly Joe's foot touched the gaping hole in the center of the room. He swiveled to one side to avoid falling into the pit and lost his balance, tumbling instead to the floor.

"This is it!" cried Derek, leaping to Joe's side and placing a foot on his chest. As Joe looked up in horror, Derek placed the end of the sword against Joe's Adam's apple.

"I'm going to finish you off for good, Hardy!"

The Hardy Boys Mystery Stories

Available from MINSTREL Books

THE HARDY BOYS® MYSTERY STORIES

DUNGEON OF DOOM

FRANKLIN W. DIXON

PUBLISHED BY POCKET BOOKS

New York   London   Toronto   Sydney   Tokyo   Singapore

A MINSTREL PAPERBACK *ORIGINAL*

A Minstrel Book, published by
POCKET BOOKS, a division of Simon & Schuster Inc.
1230 Avenue of the Americas, New York, NY 10020

Copyright © 1989 by Simon & Schuster Inc.
Cover art copyright © Paul Bachem
Produced by Mega-Books of New York, Inc.

ISBN: 0-671-69449-9

First Minstrel Books printing December 1989

10 9 8 7 6 5 4 3 2

THE HARDY BOYS MYSTERY STORIES is a trademark of Simon & Schuster Inc.

THE HARDY BOYS, A MINSTREL BOOK and colophon are registered trademarks of Simon & Schuster Inc.

Printed in the U.S.A.

Contents

DUNGEON
OF DOOM

1 The Citadel of the Serpent

"Stand back, you scurvy knaves!" shouted Chet Morton, leaping out of the front door of his house and waving a sword in the air. "Make another move and I'll run you through! 'Tis lucky for you that I left my magic amulet in my other pair of pants!"

Frank and Joe Hardy, striding up the walkway in front of Chet's house, froze in midstep and stared at their heavyset friend in astonishment. Chet was wearing a vest of aluminum foil crumpled to look like chain mail, with a silver-painted plastic helmet perched atop his head. His rubber sword vibrated like a guitar string as he waved it back and forth.

"Chet?" asked Frank tentatively. "Is that you under there?" The dark-haired eighteen-year-old turned and exchanged a glance with his blond

1

younger brother, Joe, then the two burst simultaneously into laughter.

"You look," gasped Frank, "you look—"

"—even dumber than usual!" finished Joe.

Chet gave them a pained look. "Hey, come on, guys! Show a little respect, huh? It took me two whole hours to put this outfit together!"

"That long?" Joe asked, his blue eyes open wide. "What did you make it out of? Old TV-dinner trays?"

"What's the occasion, Chet?" asked Frank. "Halloween isn't until October."

"It's for the game," said Chet. "The one I invited you over here to watch. A lot of the players wear costumes. Just call me Morton the Magnificent, Slayer of Dragons!"

Chet's sister, Iola, appeared at the door behind him. Iola was Joe's girlfriend, a pretty brunette. She cast a wary glance at her brother.

"He's been like this all week," she said, "ever since he started playing Wizards and Warriors. Maybe you guys can reason with him."

"I wouldn't count on it," said Frank with a mischievous look in his brown eyes. "When Chet gets like this, there isn't much that anybody can do."

"Wizards and Warriors is a terrific game," said Chet defensively. "You're going to love it. You'll see."

"I hope so," said Joe. "As long as you don't expect me to dress up like Unklunk the Barbarian."

"So what's this game about?" asked Frank. "I'm not sure I've heard of it before."

2

"It's what's called a role-playing game," said Chet. "You pretend to be a warrior or a sorcerer or a thief and you get to fight dragons and trolls and stuff. The Wizard Master tells you where you are and what's happening—"

"Slow down!" said Joe. "You're losing me. Who's this Wizard Master guy?"

"Come on," said Chet. "I'll show you. Some of the players are already down at the barn, waiting for us. You guys can watch us play."

"I can't wait," said Joe dryly. He turned to Iola. "Want to come along?"

"Sorry," she said with a sly smile. "Callie Shaw and I are going over to Bayport Mall for a late-afternoon shopping expedition. You're on your own. Oh, don't forget the snacks, Chet." She held a large paper bag out to her brother.

Chet's face lit up as he took it from her. "Thanks, Iola. Killing dragons is hungry work." He peered into the bag. "Let's see, we've got the potato chips, the cheese curls, the pork rinds . . ."

Joe laughed. "I should have known playing this game would make Chet think of food. *Everything* makes Chet think of food!"

"You do plan to share that with the rest of us, don't you, Chet?" asked Frank. "Chet? Hey, Chet . . .?"

With Chet leading the way, the trio made its way down the dirt path from the Morton house to the old barn around back. The barn door was open when they arrived, and a trio of teenagers was waiting inside. Two were carrying swords and the third wore an ornate bathrobe cinched at the waist with a

3

brightly colored sash. Several folding chairs had been set up around the room, and there was a large table with books and equipment stacked on top of it.

"Hey, guys!" shouted Chet in greeting. "I want you to meet my friends Frank and Joe Hardy. Frank, Joe, welcome to the GBAWWC!"

"The GBA what?" asked Frank.

"The Greater Bayport Area Wizards and Warriors Club," said the young man wearing the robe. He was about nineteen years old, of medium height, with dark brown hair and a pale complexion. He extended his hand to the brothers. "I'm Pete Simmons, the club's Wizard Master."

"There's that Wizard Master business again," said Joe. "What exactly do you Wizard Masters do, anyway?"

"Just think of me as the master of ceremonies," Pete told him. "I'll be your guide into a fantasy universe."

"That sure clears everything up," said Joe with a frown.

"This is Win Thurber," said Chet, pointing to a slender, wiry-haired boy with dark-rimmed glasses perched on a freckled face. "Win's our club know-it-all."

Win laughed. "I prefer to think of myself as the resident Wizards and Warriors expert," he said in a reedy voice. "If you've got any questions about the game, just ask me. I *live* for this game!"

"I'm sure I'll have lots of questions," said Frank. "Just wait until the game gets started."

"And this fella over here is Derek Hannon," said

4

Chet, pointing to a tall teenager with a long, aristocratic face and penetrating dark eyes, wearing a brown tunic with a coat of arms emblazoned on the front. "He's the club's champion player."

Joe's expression darkened. "Hey, I know you from somewhere, don't I?"

Derek arched an eyebrow imperiously. "Well, if it isn't old Hardhead Hardy, ace player for the Bayport High football team!"

"Now I remember you," exclaimed Joe angrily. "You play for the Littonville High team. You're the lamebrain who kicked me in the head with his cleats at the homecoming game last fall!"

"It was an accident," said Derek with a sneer, "but if I'd known then what an obnoxious twerp you are, Hardy, I'd have done it on purpose. It's not as though there's anything in your head that might get damaged."

"Why, you dumb . . . !" Joe started to lunge forward, but his brother, who was taller by one inch, was able to grab him by the shoulder before he could complete the movement.

"Whoa, boy!" Frank shouted. "Let's let bygones be bygones, huh? We're here to watch the game, not start a war!"

"I'm glad to see there's somebody in the Hardy family with smarts," said Derek. "Joe must have gotten all the recessive genes."

"Stuff it in your tunic, Hannon!" snarled Joe. "What are you doing around here, anyway? On parole from the Littonville Zoo?"

"I got tired of playing only football," said Derek,

"and thought I'd try a game that requires brains for a change. Which doesn't explain what *you're* doing here, Hardy."

"If you two could postpone this charming conversation until later," said Pete Simmons, "I'd like to get this game underway. We're starting a new scenario tonight and I'm anxious to get our party formed."

"Scenario?" asked Frank.

"It's kind of like a short story," explained Win Thurber. "Every month W&W Productions, the company that puts out the Wizards and Warriors game, publishes a magazine describing a new plot which you can base a game around. It takes our club about four weeks to play through an entire scenario. This month's is called *The Citadel of the Serpent.*"

"Unfortunately," Pete Simmons continued, "a couple of our players haven't arrived. Tim Partridge and Barry Greenwald were supposed to be here fifteen minutes ago, but they haven't shown up yet. I've never known them to be late, so I guess we'll have to assume that they aren't coming."

"Hey!" cried Chet. "I've got a great idea! Why don't we let Frank and Joe play the game in place of Tim and Barry?"

"Uh, I think I'll sit this one out and watch the rest of you play, if you don't mind," said Frank.

"Me, too," said Joe. "Just go ahead with the game. Pretend we're not here."

"What's the matter, Hardy?" asked Derek. "Afraid it might be too intellectually demanding for you?"

6

Joe threw a savage glance at Derek. "Okay, okay. I guess I'll play. Anything to shut this creep up. Where's the playing board?"

"There's no board, Joe," Pete said. "We play the game in our minds. But first we have to generate your character."

"We have to what?" asked Joe.

"I'll do it for you," said Pete. "This will just take a second." He took a pair of oddly shaped dice from the pile of equipment on the table and rolled them several times, scribbling something on a piece of paper after each roll.

"Okay, Joe. Your character has a strength of fourteen, stamina of twelve, and intelligence of three."

"Hah!" Derek laughed. "All brawn and no brains! You didn't need to roll the dice to learn that!"

"What do you want to call the character, Joe?" asked Pete.

"Huh?" said Joe, a perplexed look on his face. "I don't know. Why don't we call him Joe?"

"Make it *Sir* Joe," suggested Chet.

"Sir Joe it is," said Pete. "And now let the game begin!"

Pete settled back into a chair placed next to the table and spread open a magazine. He laced his fingers under his chin, stared ominously at the other players, and began to read.

" 'In the land of Dunadin,' " he intoned, " 'many centuries ago, there lived a great serpent named Tarag. He held the denizens of the land in his evil thrall. Crops withered when he gazed upon the

7

fields, and the sun hid behind clouds when he flew through the skies on his great wings. A savage winter fell over the land.'"

Joe gave Frank a funny look. "Is this weird or what?" he whispered.

"Shhh," said Frank. "I want to hear this."

"'The people of Dunadin lived quietly and sadly under the oppressive rule of the serpent. Yet in the village of Lodd there arose a small band of adventurers who sought to overthrow the serpent's dominion. Their names were Lord Balron—'"

Derek grinned smugly.

"'—Simon the Sorcerous—'"

Win nodded his head.

"'—Morton the Magnificent—'"

Chet took a little bow.

"'—and Sir Joe.'"

"Er, I guess that's me," said Joe. "What do we do now?"

"Patience, Sir Joe," said Pete. "You and the rest of the band of adventurers leave the village on a sunny morning attired in cloth armor and carrying daggers. You are in search of a small shop where you can purchase superior armament. As you cross the countryside, you are accosted by a band of four brigands, who threaten to slay you for the small amount of gold that you carry. Do you defend yourselves, give the brigands your gold, or flee for your lives?"

"Defend!" cried Derek. "Never retreat, never surrender, that's my motto!"

"Defend!" agreed Win, a sentiment that was echoed a second later by Chet.

"Well, Joe?" asked Pete. "Defend, surrender, or flee?"

"I, um, guess I'll defend," replied Joe.

"What now, Lord Balron?" Pete asked Derek. "One of the brigands has a sword aimed at your throat!"

"Run him through with my dagger!" cried Derek maliciously. "It'd serve him right!"

Pete rolled the dice on the table. "Good move, Lord Balron. That's one less brigand to worry about."

Joe leaned toward Win Thurber and whispered, "What's he doing with those dice?"

"The Wizard Master uses the dice to decide the result of each encounter," Win replied. "The *Wizard Master's Manual* gives the rules for using the dice, but Pete doesn't have to use it. He memorized the rules long ago."

Pete looked at Win. "How about you, Simon the Sorcerous? One of the brigands practically has his hands on your gold purse."

"I'll rub my magic amulet and recite the Fribjib spell," said Win.

"Ah, the Fribjib spell," said Pete. "That's the one that turns humans into frogs, isn't it?" He rolled the dice. "Looks like it worked, O sorcerous one! The brigand just croaked, so to speak.

"Whoops!" he added, throwing the dice yet another time. "A particularly nasty brigand just took a swipe at Morton the Magnificent and nicked him with the edge of his sword. Morton is slightly injured. What do you want to do about that, Morton?"

9

"Give him a sharp karate chop to the back of the neck," said Chet firmly.

"One karate chop, coming up," said Pete, rolling the dice yet again. "And the luckless brigand falls to the ground unconscious. Congratulations, Morton! Now it's up to you, Sir Joe. Only one brigand left and he's a mean-looking one. Better move fast!"

Joe's mouth dropped. "I, uh, well, um . . ."

"Well put, Sir Joe." Derek laughed. "I knew you'd come through in a pinch."

"I'll do the same thing *he* did," Joe announced, nodding toward Derek. "Run the brigand through with my dagger."

Pete rolled the dice. "Sorry, Sir Joe. He's too far away for your dagger to reach—and he's got a long sword. Try again before he cuts a hole in your armor."

"Well, uh," stammered Joe. "I know! Throw the dagger at him."

"Quick thinking, Sir Joe," said Pete. "And it works! The last of the brigands bites the dust. Everybody gains seven experience points.

"And what's this?" Pete added. "It looks like Sir Joe has found a bag full of treasure dropped by a brigand. Yes, indeed, Sir Joe is now five hundred gold pieces richer and has a brand-new sword. I'd say that Sir Joe has gotten the best of this encounter!"

Win Thurber slapped Joe on the shoulder. "Great work, Joe! You're catching on already."

"Huh?" said Joe, a baffled look on his face. "I mean, shucks, it was nothing."

"That about sums it up," said Derek. "Beginner's luck, Hardy."

"Don't break ranks quite yet," said Pete. "As your small band continues on its way, another enemy appears from out of the sky. It's . . . it's a baby dragon!"

"A baby dragon?" asked Joe skeptically.

"Dragons come in all shapes and sizes, Sir Joe," explained Pete. "What do you want to do?"

"I know!" said Joe. "Whack him with that brand-new sword I found!"

"Sir Joe whacks the dragon," said Pete, rolling the dice. "The dragon retaliates by breathing hot flames at Sir Joe and—uh-oh. I don't know how to tell you this, Sir Joe, but—"

"Yes?" asked Joe. "But what?"

"You're dead. Sorry about that, Sir Joe. You should show more respect for dragons."

"Dead!" shouted Joe. "What do you mean, dead? We just started the game!"

"I love it!" crowed Derek maliciously. "And at the claws of a baby dragon! He was probably too smart for you, Hardy!"

"Okay, I've had just about enough of—" Joe rounded angrily on Derek and prepared to chew him out. But his words were interrupted by a loud banging sound at the barn door. Chet rose and opened the latch. A sandy-haired boy of about fourteen stumbled inside, a frightened look on his face.

"Tim!" cried Pete Simmons. "What happened to

you? We were expecting you a half hour ago. And where's Barry Greenwald?"

The newcomer looked up with terrified eyes, his hands visibly shaking. "S-something's happened to Barry!" he stammered. "Something horrible! I think . . . I think . . ."

"Yes?" asked Win urgently. "What happened to him, Tim?"

"I think," Tim said tremulously, "that he's trapped in the Dungeon of Doom!"

2 Descent into Doom

"The Dungeon of Doom?" echoed Joc incredulously. "I think you guys are starting to take this game a little too seriously."

"What do you mean, he's in the dungeon?" Win asked Tim. "What's he doing *there?*"

"He knew we were meeting at Chet's place this afternoon," added Pete. "We won't be at the dungeon until this weekend."

"You don't understand," gasped Tim. "I think he's in trouble! I think something's gone wrong at the dungeon!"

"Slow down," said Frank. "What's this Dungeon of Doom business, anyway? Is it a real place, or another one of your imaginary scenarios?"

13

Pete, Win, and Derek exchanged glances. "Should we tell them?" Win asked.

Pete shrugged. "I guess it can't hurt. They've already heard about it . . . and, let's face it, we'd probably have invited them to the dungeon this weekend, anyway. We promised Chet we'd take him, after all. Go ahead and tell them, Win."

"Okay," said Win. "But we'd better listen to what Tim has to say first. Go ahead, Tim. Why do you think something happened to Barry?"

"I . . . I was supposed to meet Barry this after- noon in Grover Park," Tim said. "We go to school together, you know, and in math class this morning Barry told me that he thought something funny was going on in the dungeon. He wanted us to go over after school and check it out."

"What did he mean, something *funny* going on?" asked Derek.

"I'm not sure," replied Tim. "He said he'd seen some people around the dungeon. I guess he thought there might be trouble. He was going to explain the rest when we met at the park."

"He didn't show up?" Pete asked.

"No. I was going to meet him at the bench next to the statue, but when I got there I found an envelope taped to the back of the bench with my name written on it. I opened it up and found . . . this!"

He held up a letter written on plain white paper. Pete took it from him, held it where Win and Derek could see it, then handed it to Frank. There was a message written on the paper in large block letters:

14

BARRY STUCK HIS NOSE WHERE IT
DIDN'T BELONG. STAY AWAY FROM THE
DUNGEON OR YOU'LL MEET THE SAME
FATE HE DID!

Frank passed the message to Joe. "Okay," he said. "*Now* will somebody explain what this dungeon is?"

"The Dungeon of Doom is where we play Wizards and Warriors on the weekends. It's actually an old abandoned mine on the edge of town. We've fixed it up to look like a medieval dungeon, with chests full of fake treasures, big creaking doors, the works."

"That's all?" said Joe. "Why the fuss?"

"We're not exactly supposed to be there," explained Win. "The mine was shut down years ago. It was even scheduled to be sealed off once, but nobody ever got around to doing it."

"We figured it wouldn't hurt anybody if we used the mine to add a little, uh, realism to our games," Pete added.

"So why would somebody nab this kid Barry for hanging around this . . . this dungeon of yours?" asked Joe.

"Good question," said Pete. "Are you sure Barry didn't tell you anything else, Tim?"

"N-no," Tim answered. "He was going to tell me more later, but he never had the chance."

"Well," said Frank, "I know one thing. This note sounds like serious business. We'd better take it to the police."

"No!" cried Win frantically. "I mean, I don't think that's such a hot idea!"

"Why not?" said Joe. "If this friend of yours has been kidnapped, the police should be called in immediately. You don't joke around with this kind of thing."

"What Win means," said Pete, "is that if the police find out we've been using the mine as a setting for our games, they'll throw us out for good. That old mine is condemned property. Nobody's allowed in there."

"And if they knew we'd been using it," Win continued, "they'd board the place up tighter than a drum. They'd never let us back inside."

"I don't believe I'm hearing this!" Frank said, shaking his head. "Your friend may be in desperate trouble right now, and you're worried about being able to play this game of yours!"

"Maybe Barry's playing a joke on us," Pete suggested. "All we have to do is drive out to the dungeon and take a look around. I bet Barry jumps up and yells 'Surprise' the moment we walk in."

"Sure," said Win. "Just a joke! That's all it is!"

"I don't think so," said Tim darkly. "He sounded pretty serious . . . and Barry isn't really that big on jokes. I think these guys are right. We ought to go to the police."

"I've got an idea," said Derek. "We'll go to the police . . . as soon as we check out the dungeon. Like Pete says, all we have to do is drive over and take a look around. If Barry isn't there, we call the police. Agreed?"

Frank shrugged. "I'm not crazy about the idea."

"Neither am I," agreed Joe.

"It'll take no time at all," said Pete. "We can be at the dungeon in twenty minutes. Let's all drive together."

"I'd better not come along," said Tim. "My mother's expecting me home early."

"The rest of us will go, then," said Win. "The six of us."

Joe sighed. "All right. You win. We've got a van parked out front. I'll drive."

"And I've got a battery-operated lantern in the trunk of my car," offered Derek. "We'll need it in the dungeon."

"I'll bring the snacks!" cried Chet.

"Good old Chet," said Frank wryly. "What would we do without you?"

Twenty minutes later, the van turned down a seldom-used road on the outskirts of Bayport. Pete motioned toward a dense patch of trees, and Joe pulled the Hardy van onto the shoulder of the road.

"We'll have to walk from here," Pete told the Hardys. "It's not far, but the woods are pretty thick. We've never cleared a path through them. We were afraid that somebody might accidentally stumble onto the dungeon if we did."

"If this used to be a working mine," said Frank, "shouldn't the entrance be easier to reach?"

"This wasn't the main entrance," said Pete.

"Right," said Win. "The main entrance is under about twenty feet of water."

"What?" exclaimed Joe.

Pete laughed. "Bayport Reservoir is just on the other side of these woods. That's why they closed

17

the mine. When they built the reservoir, it flooded the lower chambers. We've never been that far down, of course. We enter the mine through one of the upper shafts, which nobody ever bothered to close off."

"It's through these woods," Derek said to Joe. "Come on, Hardy. Show me that pioneer spirit!"

The group plunged into the thick of the woods, pushing aside tangled branches and stumbling through heavy undergrowth. Finally, they came to a small clearing, where sunlight filtered through the trees in splotchy patches. Pete brushed away a net of dead limbs to reveal a roughly circular hole in the ground, several feet wide.

"I think this was some kind of emergency exit," Pete said. "There's a ladder inside. One of the main rooms of the mine is about ten feet down. Derek, you've got the lantern, so you can go first."

Derek nodded, then lowered his feet into the hole. After a few seconds of climbing, he disappeared into the ground. Pete and Win followed. Frank, Joe, and Chet exchanged glances.

"You're not getting *me* inside there!" exclaimed Chet.

"I doubt that you'd fit." Joe laughed. "The hole's only wide enough to hold a small Buick."

Chet looked indignant. "What do you mean, I wouldn't fit? Watch this!"

The heavyset teenager hunkered down by the side of the hole. He dangled his feet inside until they caught a rung of the ladder, then he jiggled his way downward.

"Tight squeeze?" asked Joe.

"Lots of room," replied Chet. "Uh, you guys want to hold my sword until we get down there?" He held his rubber sword out to Frank, who took it from him. Then he descended into the hole.

"You going down, too?" Joe asked Frank.

"If Chet can do it, so can I," said Frank.

"Then let's go," said Joe. One after the other, the two brothers clambered into the hole in pursuit of the Wizards and Warriors players.

After climbing about ten feet straight down, Frank's foot touched solid ground. Lowering himself off the last rung of the ladder, he took a long look at his surroundings.

At first he could not see anything. Then, as his eyes adjusted to the dark, he could make out the dim glow of Derek's lantern. The group was standing in a large room, with walls of rock and clay and a low dirt ceiling. Old wooden braces were faintly visible through the dirt, but someone had painted them dark gray to blend in with the walls.

At the near end of the room, where the ladder emerged from the entrance, the ceiling sloped to within a few feet of the ground. Stooping low, Frank walked to the other side of the room, where the ceiling was higher and the remaining members of the group stood clustered together. Seconds later, Joe joined him.

"Welcome to the Dungeon of Doom!" said Win.

Scattered around the room were several wooden trunks, painted to look like pirate chests from an old movie. Colorful tapestries hung on two of the walls.

19

Set into the wall opposite the ladder were three massive-looking doors with oversize keyholes. Each door had a coat of arms painted on it.

"This was one of the main galleries of the mine," Pete explained. "Three tunnels branch off from here, going deeper into the ground. As you can see, we've added a bit of our own decor to the place."

"Wow!" said Joe. "This is pretty impressive! This must be a great place to play Wizards and Warriors. But how could you guys afford to set something like this up?"

"Oh, it wasn't hard," said Win. "I've, ah, got connections in the retail trade."

Pete laughed. "Win has a part-time job at a department store," he said. "He can get things at a discount. Lumber, paint, stuff like that. We built the chests ourselves, out of cheap wood. The tapestries are just old bed sheets. The doors are factory rejects, but they're very sturdy."

"What about the locks on the doors?" asked Frank. "Afraid that somebody might break in?"

"There aren't any locks. Or any keys," said Derek. "Here, I'll show you."

Derek walked to one of the doors and gave the handle a tug. It failed to budge. He turned to the others with a startled look on his face.

"They're not *supposed* to be locked," he said in a baffled tone. "They've never been locked before."

"Let me give it a try," said Pete. "It's probably just jammed."

He reached out and gripped the doorhandle with

20

both hands, pulling on it firmly. The door rattled slightly but remained closed.

"I don't understand," said Pete. "Something must have happened to the door. Win, try one of the others."

Win walked to the middle door and pulled on the handle. "It's locked," he said. "And I'll bet the last door is, too."

"You win the bet," said Frank, pulling on the handle of the third door. "Are these the only ways out of this room?"

"I'm afraid so," said Pete. "Except for the exit, of course. But that just takes us back outside." He frowned. "This is going to make it awfully hard to look for Barry."

"I wonder if this has something to do with his disappearance," mused Frank. "When's the last time you guys were down here?"

"Last weekend," said Win. "The doors were okay then."

"Maybe we can break the doors down," said Joe.

"Not very likely," said Win. "We worked for weeks to make these doors secure. You'd need a jackhammer to get those things back down."

"Is there another entrance to the mine?" asked Frank.

"No," said Derek. "Not above water, anyway."

Pete clenched a fist in anger. "I guess you guys were right. We'll have to go to the police after all."

"Come on," said Derek with a sigh, walking back toward the ladder. "Let's get out of here."

21

"Hold on!" said Win suddenly. "What's that? I've never seen it before."

He reached behind one of the chests and pulled out what looked to be a roll of yellowing paper with a cloth ribbon tied around it. Win pulled a small knife from his pocket and cut the ribbon, then unrolled the paper.

"It looks like a scroll," said Pete.

"There's something written on it," said Win.

"What does it say?" asked Frank.

"It's a poem," said Win. "It says,

"'WELCOME TO THE DUNGEON.
NOW TAKE A DEEP BREATH.
ONE DOOR LEADS TO TREASURE,
THE OTHERS TO DEATH.'"

Joe laughed. "You've got to be kidding."

"Here," said Win. "Take a look at it your—"

The end of Win's sentence was drowned out by a resounding explosion. Rocks and dirt gushed down into the mine, where the entrance had been. Both the ladder and the hole leading upward vanished under a pile of rubble. Clouds of dust billowed into the air.

"What the—?" shouted Frank.

"It's a cave-in!" cried Pete in a panicky voice, barely audible above the rumble of falling rocks. "The entrance is gone! We're trapped!"

22

3 Trapped!

A babble of panicky voices rose above the fading echoes of the explosion. For several seconds everyone seemed to be speaking at the same time.

"Trapped?" shouted Joe.

"We can't be trapped!" yelled Win. "I don't believe it."

"What will we *do?*" wailed Pete.

"Don't panic, that's what!" yelled Frank, cutting through the uproar. "Everybody stay calm. There's got to be another way out of this place!"

The dust from the rockslide settled slowly as the echoes of the explosion died away. Win sneezed and Pete coughed loudly. Frank waved his hand in front of his face to scatter the dust cloud. Joe stared at the fallen rocks as though stunned.

"What in the world happened?" he asked finally. "It sounded like an explosion!"

"Maybe," said Win. "Or maybe it was just a rockslide. We could have triggered it on the way down. This mine has been around since the turn of the century. It might not be as safe as we thought."

Pete knelt in front of the pile of rocks where the entrance had been. "The ladder's completely buried," he said. "No way can we get to it. We've got about ten tons of rock in the way."

"We'll never get past that," said Frank. "I guess we'll just have to find another exit."

"There isn't another exit," moaned Win. "We're trapped!"

"Terrific," muttered Derek. "I should have had my head examined when I helped you guys fix up this place. I must have been crazy!"

"You've got my vote on that," agreed Joe. "If you're so smart, Derek, why don't you think up a way out of here? In fact, how do we know that *you're* not the one responsible for that rockslide? It was your idea that we come here in the first place. Maybe you set this up to trap us."

"Why in the world would I do that, jerk?" Derek's voice rose as he glared at Joe. "I don't have any reason to want us trapped here. Haven't you noticed that I'm trapped, too? As for a way out, there isn't one. Not that we know about, anyway."

"I don't know why you'd want us trapped here," said Joe, "but I don't trust you for a second. I'll be keeping my eyes on you, Hannon."

"You've really got me worried, Hardy." Derek laughed. "I've heard about that hotshot-detective reputation that you and your brother are supposed to have. I'll bet you couldn't find a snowball at the North Pole—in the middle of February."

"Oh, no!" shouted Chet abruptly, his voice rising in horror. "This is terrible, really terrible!"

The others spun around to face him. "What is it, Chet?" asked Frank. "Don't tell me something else has happened!"

"Something *terrible* has happened!" cried Chet mournfully. "I left the snacks out in the van! I'm going to starve!"

"Oh, brother!" groaned Joe. "Can't you *ever* get your mind off your stomach, Chet?"

"He may have a point," said Frank. "We're all going to get a little hungry as time goes on. There's no telling how long we're going to be down here."

"Somebody'll dig us out," said Pete. "Tim Partridge knows we're here. He'll have to tell the authorities."

"Tim Partridge is sworn to secrecy about this place." Win's voice was a little shaky. "He'd sooner give away his collection of old comic books than tell the police about the dungeon."

"If we're missing long enough, he'll have to tell somebody, whether he wants to or not," said Derek. "It'll be obvious that something's gone wrong."

"Sure," said Pete. "After we don't show up for three or four days."

"And it'll take three or four more days to dig us out," said Joe. "We could die of dehydration before then."

"I could die of starvation!" moaned Chet. "I didn't even bring a candy bar!"

"What did you say about an exit?" Frank asked Derek. "You said that there was no exit that you 'know about.' Did you mean that there might be an exit that you guys *don't* know about?"

"It's possible," agreed Derek. "We've never explored the whole place."

"That's right," said Pete. "We've stayed away from the lower tunnels of the mine. Supposedly they're flooded with water from the reservoir, but we've never been down there. For all we know, the mine could be riddled with exits."

"Then I think we'd better start looking for them," said Frank. "The sooner, the better."

"What about those locked doors?" asked Joe. "If we can't get them open, we'll be spending the next week in this room. And I doubt that there's enough air to go around. It already smells pretty stale in here."

"I'll second that," said Chet with a cough.

"Then we'll have to find something that'll get us through the doors," said Frank, glancing around the room. "What's in these chests, anyway?"

"Nothing, at the moment," said Win. "During the games, we fill them with treasures—fake jewelry, play money, that sort of thing. We give out points to the player who finds the most goodies during a game."

"Well, we might as well take a look in one of them," said Frank, kneeling next to one of the chests. "Maybe you left something inside that we can use. How do you open these things?"

"Just move that metal hook to one side and the top

will come open," explained Win. "There, you've got it."

Frank popped open the top of the chest and peered inside. "Hey, there *is* something useful in here!"

He pulled an oversize skeleton key from the chest and held it up for the others to see. It was painted bright red.

"Where did that come from?" asked Pete.

"Don't look at me," replied Derek. "*I've* never seen it before."

"Maybe that opens one of the doors," said Joe.

"It wouldn't hurt to try," said Frank.

"Hey, look at that," said Derek, pointing at the door on the left. The keyhole had been painted a vivid blue.

"Somebody's painted the keyholes on the doors different colors," Derek said. "The keyhole on that door is bright blue . . ."

"That one's green," said Pete, looking at the middle door.

"And this one is red," said Frank, pointing to the door on the right. "Just like the key I found."

"Why don't you try the key in that door?" suggested Joe.

"My thought exactly," said Frank. He walked to the door on the right, plunged the key into the red keyhole, and turned it. The lock clicked. When Frank pulled on the door, it opened easily, revealing a gaping darkness beyond.

"Check it out!" Frank declared. "We're on our way!"

"If there's a red key," said Joe, "there must be a green key and a blue key, too, to fit the locks on the other two doors. Let's check the other two trunks."

Win opened the trunk next to him. "You're right," he said, reaching inside. "Here's the blue key."

"And here's the green one," added Derek, opening the third trunk. "Maybe we're not trapped after all."

A strange look passed over Win's face. "Do you realize what's happening here?" he said.

"Huh?" said Joe. "What are you talking about?"

"This is a game of Wizards and Warriors," Win said. "A real-life game, not an imaginary one. The locked doors. The keys. The scroll. It's just like something out of the game, except that it's really happening."

"You're right." Pete frowned in thought. "That scroll you found a minute ago . . . someone must have deliberately left that here for us to find. And whoever wrote the scroll must be the same person who blocked the exit."

"The Secret Wizard Master!" said Win with mounting excitement in his voice.

"What?" said Frank. "Pete's the Wizard Master. Are you suggesting that *he* did this to us?"

Win shook his head. "No. I'm suggesting that there's a *secret* Wizard Master behind what's happening, somebody who's playing a game of Wizards and Warriors with us for our lives. I don't know who he is or why he's doing it, but it makes a horrible kind of sense. He locked the doors, but he also hid

28

the keys in the chests. He's testing us, to see how well we can play his game. And I'll bet he's got a few more tricks up his sleeve."

"But what's his motive?" asked Derek. "Why doesn't he just show up at one of the regular game sessions and play for fun? If you ask me, trapping a bunch of guys in an old mine is a pretty sick way to get your kicks."

"Sounds like the kind of thing *you'd* do," said Joe, with a glance at Derek.

"We'll just have to keep our eyes and ears open," Frank said, intervening before Derek could respond in kind. "If there *is* a secret Wizard Master, maybe he's left a few clues to his identity. Or a few clues to how we can get out of here."

"The scroll said something about one of these doors leading to treasure," said Joe. "Maybe the treasure is the exit."

"Could be," said Frank. "Where do these doors go, anyway?"

"Each door leads into a separate tunnel from the old mine," said Pete. "We've never been to the end of any of them."

"Okay," said Frank. "Let's explore the tunnels one at a time. Since we've already got the door on the right open, let's try that tunnel first. Everybody ready? Who wants to lead?"

The six teenagers stared at one another for a moment, then Win spoke up. "I know this place pretty well. Follow me."

Win took the lantern from Derek and stepped to

29

the door. Standing on the threshold, he held the lantern out in front of him and peered into the next room.

"It looks safe," he announced. "Let's go in."

The group followed Win through the door. The next room was much smaller than the first room, about fifteen feet long and ten feet wide. In the middle of the floor lay an ornate green carpet, beyond which sat another wooden chest. On the wall above the chest was a coat of arms with two swords crossed underneath it. Next to the coat of arms was another door, this one with a keyhole painted gray.

"Wow!" said Joe. "Pretty nice setup! I like that stuff on the wall. And where'd you get that carpet?"

"It's an old rug my parents were throwing out," said Pete. "We painted it to look like an oriental carpet. You should see it in the daylight."

"You *shouldn't* see it in the daylight," said Win. "It looks like something the cat dragged in."

"Well, I'm going to take a look in that chest," said Joe. "Maybe we can find more keys inside."

Joe walked toward the chest, stepping on the carpet. Suddenly the carpet gave way and the floor seemed to vanish from underneath Joe's feet.

A black pit opened up beneath the carpet. With a shout, Joe plunged into the yawning darkness!

4 Tokens of Power

For a few seconds, it seemed to Joe as if the world had turned upside down. The floor beneath his feet had been replaced by a dark hole as black as the night sky . . . and he was falling into it!

He flailed his hands around, trying to find support. At first he grabbed only air. Then his hands struck some kind of wooden bar so hard that the pain of the impact shot through his arms and into his body. He closed his eyes in shock, tightly gripping whatever it was that his hands had struck. His ears rang loudly.

"Joe! Hey, Joe!" shouted a voice somewhere above him. "Are you okay?"

He looked up to see his brother, Frank, staring down at him. Next to Frank stood Chet, holding the lantern.

"Uh, yeah," said Joe dully. "I . . . I think so. What happened?"

Frank and Chet exchanged glances. "You fell in some kind of pit. Hang on. We'll get you out."

Joe looked to see what it was that his arms had grabbed. In the dim light, it appeared to be a piece of an old wooden ladder, attached to the earthen lining of the pit by rusty metal bolts. He had wrapped his arms almost completely around the bottom rung—his feet were dangling in midair. He looked down to see how deep the pit was, but could see only darkness. Far below, he could hear the sound of running water.

Glancing up, he saw Frank and Chet staring down at him, from what seemed like a very long distance but was probably no more than four or five feet. "Hey, you guys!" Joe yelled in a shaky voice. "Some of the rungs are missing from this ladder. You're gonna have to help me get out."

"Hang on, Joe," said Frank. "We'll have you out in a flash." He turned to Win. "Give me that rope you've got wrapped around your tunic. We'll use it to pull Joe out."

"I don't know if it's strong enough," said Win, pulling the rope from around his waist. "Or long enough."

"We'd better hope that it's both of those things," said Frank. "Give me a hand, Chet."

Frank lowered one end of the rope into the pit. "Chet and I will hold on to this end of the rope," he said to Joe, "but you're going to have to climb up by yourself. You're too heavy to pull."

"I can't reach it!" said Joe, grabbing at the rope

with one hand while holding onto the bottom rung of the ladder with the other. "Keep lowering it!"

"That's as low as it will go," replied Frank. "Push yourself up on that rung. You can reach the rope if you try."

"Easy for you to say," gasped Joe, but he did as Frank suggested, pushing himself upward as far as he could with his right arm. His fingers wiggled just beneath the tip of the rope. With a burst of strength he pushed himself a little higher—and his hand closed around the rope.

"Got it!" he shouted. "You guys pull as hard as you can, okay?"

"Okay," said Frank. "Just keep pushing on that ladder!"

With a grunt, Joe pushed free of the ladder and grabbed the rope with both hands. Frank and Chet pulled frantically at their end of the rope as Joe scrabbled up the sheer wall of the pit, pushing at the fragments of the ladder with his feet to propel himself upward.

Finally he got his arms over the edge of the pit. Frank and Chet grabbed him by his shoulders and pulled him back onto solid ground.

"Whew!" said Frank. "I thought we'd lost you there for a minute! Lucky you caught that ladder."

"Real lucky," said Joe, his voice a little ragged. "I think I'd better sit down for a minute and, uh, catch my breath."

"Take your time," said Frank. "You look pretty shook-up."

"I feel pretty shook-up," said Joe. "But I'll be okay in a minute."

"What was that hole Joe fell in?" Frank asked the others. "Are there more of those down here?"

"It was a mine shaft," said Pete. "Tunnels run horizontally and shafts run straight up and down. Yes, there are more of them around. I thought we'd covered that one up a long time ago, so nobody would get hurt."

"Obviously someone uncovered it. Probably our friend the Secret Wizard Master."

"At least he knows how to run an exciting game," said Win.

"*Real* exciting," said Frank. "I can live without this much excitement, thank you. Come on, you guys. Let's sit down and take a break while Joe recovers from that fall. We might not get a lot of chances to rest down here."

"Okay with me," said Pete.

"Me, too," echoed Win, retying the rope around his tunic.

"Count me in," agreed Chet.

The group sat in a circle on the floor of the room, as far from the mine shaft as they could get. Derek and Win took their swords and laid them across their laps. Joe sprawled limply on the floor next to the others.

"As long as we've got the time," said Frank, "why don't we learn a little more about each other? Pete, why don't you tell us what it is you do when you're not playing Wizards and Warriors."

"Well," said Pete, "most of the guys in the group already know as much about me as they probably want to, but I guess you and Joe have some catching up to do. I'm a student at Gates College in Brookville. I'm majoring in psychology."

"How did you get involved with Wizards and Warriors?" Frank asked.

"I've always been interested in fantasy, science fiction, that kind of thing. I read all the Tolkien books when I was a kid. About four years ago I started reading about this new type of game, called a role-playing game. And there was this one game called Wizards and Warriors that sounded really terrific. I couldn't wait to play it. It was a chance to build a fantasy world just like the one I'd read about in *The Lord of the Rings*."

"So you found a group of people who were already playing the game?" asked Chet.

"No," said Pete. "I tried to, but nobody in this area seemed to be playing it yet. So I put a classified ad in the newspaper, asking if anybody else wanted to play. I got a few responses and that was the start of the GBAWWC."

"Tell them about the paper you're writing for your psychology professor," prompted Win.

Pete blushed. "Uh, no, I'm sure these guys don't want to hear about that."

"Oh, come on," urged Win. "I thought it sounded great!"

"Yeah, tell us about it, Pete," said Chet.

"I think I'd like to hear about it, too," said Derek.

35

"Um, okay," said Pete tentatively. "It's for my class on developmental psychology. It's entitled 'The Role-Playing Game as Adolescent Bonding Ritual.'"

Derek sat up straight. "The role-playing game as *what?*" he shouted. "Are you calling me an adolescent?"

"Yeah," said Chet. "That makes us sound like a bunch of dumb kids!"

"Well, we *are* a bunch of kids," said Win. "It sounds okay to me."

"Sounds like you're pulling rank as the group's only college student," said Derek suspiciously.

"No, it's nothing like that," said Pete defensively. "I had to write a paper for the class and I thought it would be nice to write about something I know. And what I know is role-playing games."

"Are you doing research on us when we're not looking?" asked Derek.

"Yeah—are we your guinea pigs or something?" added Chet.

"Come on, guys." Pete sighed. "It's just a paper I'm writing for a class."

"Go easy on him," said Frank. "You're all Pete's friends. I'm sure he's not using you as guinea pigs. He's just using you to get better grades."

"Well, that's a weight off my mind!" Derek chuckled.

"Now, what about you, Derek?" asked Frank. "What do you do when you're not in the group? Maybe we can find some skeletons in your closet, too."

"Probably a whole cemetery in there," said Joe, looking up from where he lay sprawled on the floor.

Derek ignored the comment. "I'm a student at Littonville High, as your brother, Joe, here already knows. I'm captain of the football team, president of the debating club, and I'll probably be class valedictorian when I graduate."

Joe made a face. "Are you looking for a cure for cancer in your spare time?"

"I play Wizards and Warriors in my spare time," said Derek irritably. "It's *usually* a fun way to relax."

"What are you going to do after you graduate from high school?" asked Frank.

"I've got scholarships to both M.I.T. and Harvard. I've narrowed my field of study down to either physics or molecular biology, with a double minor in computer science and philosophy."

"I think I'm going to be sick," said Joe.

"I'm impressed," said Frank. "You're a man of many talents."

"I happen to be good at a few things," agreed Derek.

"So how did *you* get into playing Wizards and Warriors?"

"A girlfriend of mine at Littonville High was a member of the group. She talked me into joining. I thought it sounded pretty silly at first, but before I knew it I was hooked."

"What happened to the girlfriend?" asked Chet.

"Oh, we broke up a few months ago, then she moved away to Connecticut. No big deal. She was hardly my intellectual equal."

37

"A gerbil would be your intellectual equal, Hannon," muttered Joe snidely.

"Compared to you, Hardy, a gerbil is an intellectual giant," said Derek. He turned back to Frank. "Is your brother always this nasty?"

"Only on alternate Tuesdays," said Frank. "And you can't say you haven't been asking for it all afternoon, Derek."

"Well, I just thought the twerp needed to be put in his place a few times."

"I think you've accomplished what you set out to do," Frank said. "Now why don't you and Joe bury the hatchet for a while?"

Joe sat up abruptly. "I'll bury the hatchet all right!" he said. "You get one guess where I plan to bury it!"

"Just try it, Hardy," said Derek, lunging in Joe's direction.

Frank grabbed Derek by the arm. "Calm down, you guys! We're already in a bad enough mess without the two of you trying to kill each other. Why don't you and Joe cooperate long enough to get us out of this place? *Then* you can kill each other!"

"Fine with me," said Derek. "But you ought to be asking your brother here."

"Joe?" asked Frank. "Think you two can stay away from each other's throats for a few more hours?"

"Or days," said Pete ruefully. "No telling how long we'll be down here."

"I'll lay off him if he'll lay off me," said Joe finally.

"Okay," said Frank. "It's a deal. You two have just made a truce. Now let's finish getting to know each other, so that we can get back to finding a way out. Who's next?"

"You already know all about me," said Chet. "I've known you and Joe since you were wearing diapers."

A sly smile crept across Derek's face. Frank held out the palm of his hand toward him, making a halt sign. "No comments about how recently Joe was wearing diapers, Derek!" said Frank firmly.

"I wasn't thinking any such thing," said Derek innocently.

"Right," said Frank. "Okay, Win. It's your turn. Tell us what you're like when you're not being Simon the Sorcerous."

"You don't really want to know about my life," said Win reluctantly. "It's really pretty boring."

"That's why Win likes Wizards and Warriors so much," said Pete. "It's a way of escaping from boring reality."

"Exactly!" said Win excitedly. "It's such a great game! When we finish a game I don't even want to go home. I just want to keep playing. Real life just isn't very interesting."

"Sure it is, Win," said Frank. "You've just got to *make* it interesting, that's all. You can't play games all your life."

"Why not?"

"You just can't," said Frank. "There must be something you do when you're not playing. Didn't somebody say you worked at a department store?"

"Yeah," said Win resignedly. "I work at Berg-meyer's Department Store in Bayport Mall, when I'm not going to Bayport High."

39

"You're a student at Bayport High?" asked Joe. "I've never noticed you around."

"Nobody ever does." Win sighed. "I just don't get involved in things, like you guys. *Everybody's* heard of the Hardy boys."

"You got involved with Wizards and Warriors," said Frank.

Win's eyes lit up. "Best thing I ever did," he said. "I've always been into games. Board games. War games. Computer games. I play them all."

"How did you find out about the Wizards and Warriors club?"

"Somebody at school mentioned it to me. I went to the next meeting . . . and I haven't missed one meeting since."

"Win's our most enthusiastic player," said Pete.

"He's *almost* as good a player as I am," said Derek loftily.

"I'm almost embarrassed to admit," added Pete, "that he knows more about the game than I do—and *I'm* the Wizard Master. I think he's memorized the manual."

"I have!" said Win with a smile. "Do you want to hear the section about the different classes of armor and weapons?"

"Uh, not right now," said Frank hastily. "Maybe later. Well, I guess everybody's had a chance to introduce himself. . . ."

"Why are you asking all these questions, Frank?" asked Derek. "You're not just curious, are you?"

"What do you mean?" said Frank.

"You've been pumping us for information, right? I'll bet you think one of us is the Secret Wizard Master, don't you?"

Frank nodded. "Good deduction, Derek. That's right. I think somebody in this room is responsible for us being trapped down here, and I'm trying to figure out who."

"But," said Derek, "as I pointed out earlier, we're *all* trapped down here. If the Secret Wizard Master is one of us, then he's trapped, too."

"Not necessarily," said Frank. "If we're right about there being another way out of here, the Secret Wizard Master must already know what it is. He can get out any time he wants to. And he knows where all the traps are, too."

"Why would he take the risk?" asked Pete. "It's a pretty dangerous place down here."

"He wants to be around for the game," said Frank. "After going to all the trouble to set this up, he isn't going to miss out on the fun."

"I hate to say it," said Win, "but that makes sense. So which one of us is it?"

"I don't know yet," said Frank. "I don't suppose the Secret Wizard Master would like to confess his identity, would he?"

"He's not me," said Pete.

"Me, neither," said Win.

"Nor me," said Derek.

"Or me!" said Chet.

"Well, we know one thing about the Secret Wizard Master," said Joe.

"What's that?" asked Frank.

"That he's a liar!" said Joe.

"Good point," Frank said, laughing. "Okay, I guess we'd better get moving. Feel better now, Joe?"

"Yeah," said Joe. "I was just shook-up. Let's head on to the next room."

"We haven't finished with this one yet," said Win. "We almost forgot about the chest."

"Right," said Joe. "I was about to open it when I fell into the shaft. It's okay with me if *you* open it, Win."

"Be glad to," said Win, kneeling beside the chest. "Hey, there's another one of those scrolls stuck to the back of the chest."

"What does it say?" someone asked.

Win read aloud:

> "'THE DUNGEON OF DOOM
> IS DARKER THAN NIGHT.
> THESE TOKENS OF POWER
> WILL GIVE YOU LIGHT.'"

"Wow," said Chet. "This is getting stranger and stranger."

"Open up the chest, Win," said Pete. "Let's see what's inside."

"I'm opening it," said Win, pulling the latch on the front of the chest. He raised the lid and reached inside.

"Aha!" he said. "The tokens of power!" He held up a plastic pack containing a large battery.

"I'll be darned," said Derek. "That's the size that fits my lantern."

"I guess the Secret Wizard Master expects us to be down here for a while," said Frank. "Nice of him to leave us something useful like a battery."

"Why couldn't he leave us something useful like food?" asked Chet.

"How did he just happen to know what size battery fits your lantern?" asked Joe suspiciously.

"We use this same lantern every week," said Derek. "Everybody in the group is familiar with this lantern. If you're trying to suggest that I planted that battery in that chest . . ."

"He's suggesting nothing of the sort," said Frank pointedly. "You two have a truce, remember?"

"If Mr. Perfect here turns out to be the Secret Wizard Master," said Joe, "all bets are off. I'm personally going to drop-kick him down a mine shaft."

"Okay," said Frank. "But until then, just cool off. Is everybody ready to go to the next room?"

"I think we'll need this," said Win, reaching into the chest a second time and pulling out a large gray key.

"It matches the lock on the door," said Pete.

"Then I'll lead the way," said Win, handing the battery to Derek and bounding toward the door.

"Be careful, Win," said Frank. "We don't know what's waiting for us in there."

"Don't worry," said Win, unlocking the door. "I can watch out for myself."

43

He swung the door open. Beyond it was more darkness.

Suddenly, an instant after the door was opened, an object came flying out of the darkness. It was a metal ball, suspended from the ceiling by a wire, with sharp spikes sticking out all over it.

And it was heading straight for Win and Frank!

5 The Road Not Taken

"Win! Look out!" Frank leapt at the slender young man and knocked him aside with a sharp blow from his shoulder. Win gasped as the spike ball swooshed past his cheek, then he hit the ground on one knee. Frank tumbled to the ground, next to him.

"Heads up!" shouted Joe. "That thing's still on the loose!"

The spike ball swung out to the farthest extent of its wire, swept through a wide circle, and headed back toward the door, nearly hitting Pete in the process.

"Somebody grab that thing!" shouted Pete frantically.

"*You* grab it!" replied Chet. "I'm not going anywhere near it!"

"Just stay out of its way," said Derek. "It'll lose its momentum in a few seconds. If you don't go near the door, it can't hit you."

Sure enough, when the spike ball swung back into the room a second time, it went only half as far as it had the first time. By the third swing, it seemed little more dangerous than the pendulum on a grandfather clock.

Frank rose cautiously to his feet, holding out a hand to help Win up from the floor. "Looks like the Secret Wizard Master is playing for keeps. How did he rig that thing up, anyway?"

Joe grabbed the wire on the now slow-moving spike ball. "Looks pretty simple," he said. "There are a couple of pieces of broken plastic wire attached to this ball. He must have hooked one wire to the door and the other to the far side of the room. When Win opened the door, it snapped the wire going to the far side of the room and pulled the ball into this room. An easy trap to set up, but deadly."

"Like the mine shaft you fell into," said Frank.

"Yeah. I guess we'll have to keep our guard up in this place. No telling what other traps our friend has waiting for us."

"Think it's safe now to go into the next room?" asked Pete.

"We don't have much choice," said Frank. "Still feel like leading the way, Win?"

"S-sure." Win gulped. "I'm not going to let a little thing like a spiked ball scare me."

"Why not?" asked Frank. "It scared the stuffing out of me."

46

"I just hope there's not a second trap in this doorway," said Win, taking the lantern from Derek and thrusting it through the door. "It *looks* safe. In fact, I don't see anything in this room at all."

"Not even a chest?" asked Joe.

"Not even a chest." Win slowly entered the room, the lantern held out in front of him. "Just another door."

"What color is the keyhole?" asked Frank, entering the room after Win.

"It looks . . . it looks purple," said Win.

"Anybody see a purple key?" asked Frank.

"No," said Pete. "Not in any of the rooms we've been in so far."

"And there's no chest in this room," said Joe, stepping through the door, "so there are probably no keys in here. What do we do now?"

"I don't know," said Frank. "We can't go any farther without a key."

"There were two more passages leading out of the first room," said Derek. "I say that we go back and explore a different one."

"Sounds good to me," said Win.

"I guess we don't have any other choice," said Frank.

"Then let's go," agreed Joe.

Slowly, the group made its way back to the first room. Frank stepped to the middle door, the one with its keyhole painted bright green.

"Who's got the green key?" he asked.

"I do," said Derek. "And I'll lead the way into the next room."

"Here, Chet," Win said, "you hold the lantern while Derek opens the door."

Chet took the lantern. "I hope this doesn't mean I have to stand in front of that door while he opens it."

"No," said Derek. "You stand to that side and I'll stand to this. Be ready to duck."

"I'm about ready to dig my way back to the surface," said Chet, "with my bare hands."

"You could always eat your way back to the surface," suggested Joe. "Not much protein in solid rock, but there should be a lot of minerals."

"I was thinking about that," said Chet.

Derek slid the key into the lock and turned it. "Okay," he said. "The key fits. I felt the door unlock. Everybody out of the way while I open it."

He pulled on the handle, keeping the bulk of the door between himself and the next room. Even after the door was completely open, the group stood quietly, waiting to see if something was going to happen. Nothing did.

"Well, here goes," said Derek. "Follow me with the lantern, Chet." He stepped around the door and walked slowly into the next room. Chet followed.

The room was nearly empty. On the far wall were two doors, one with a black keyhole, the other with a white one. Posted on the wall between the doors was another scroll with two keys dangling from it, one black and one white.

"Those must be the keys to the doors," said Joe. "Which one should we use?"

"We'd better read the scroll first," said Frank. "What does it say, Derek?"

Derek scanned the scroll. "It says that one of the doors is safe to open, but that there's a canister of poison gas behind the other, rigged to flood the dungeon with deadly fumes when the door is opened."

"Terrific," said Win. "How do we know which door is which?"

"There's a poem," said Derek. "Listen to this:

" 'ONE KEY BLACK AS NIGHT.
ONE KEY WHITE AS SNOW.
BING CROSBY AND SIR LANCELOT
WOULD KNOW WHICH WAY TO GO.' "

"What does that mean?" said Chet.

"It sounds like a riddle," said Frank. "What do Bing Crosby and Sir Lancelot have to do with black and white keys?"

Pete snapped his fingers. "Bing Crosby sang 'White Christmas'!"

"Hey, that's one of my favorite songs!" said Chet. " 'I'm dreaming of a'—ouch!" He rubbed his ribs where Joe had poked him. "Why'd you do that?"

Joe shook his head. "The echoes in this room make it sound like there are four of you . . . and one of you sounds bad enough!"

Chet looked hurt. "I'll have you know that the school music teacher told me I have a great voice."

"Sure, for an asthmatic frog," suggested Joe.

"Let's worry about these keys, not about Chet's singing voice," said Frank.

"That scroll must mean that we should use the

white key," said Win. " 'White Christmas,' white key."

"What about Sir Lancelot?" asked Pete. "What does he have to do with white keys?"

"Nothing," said Derek. "Sir Lancelot was a knight."

"As in 'black as night,' like the other key," said Frank. "Which puts us back where we started."

"That's a real helpful scroll," said Joe. "How do we know which key to use?"

"We don't," said Frank. "I think the Secret Wizard Master is pulling a fast one on us."

"So what do we do?" asked Pete. "Open a door at random?"

"What else can we do?" said Frank. "We can't just stand here. We have to keep looking for an exit."

"We can flip a coin," said Chet, pulling a nickel from his pocket. "Heads we choose the white keyhole, tails the black."

He tossed the coin into the air, caught it in one hand, then slapped it onto the back of his other hand.

"Heads it is," he said. "We take the white one."

"We have a fifty percent chance of getting a face full of poison gas when we open the door," said Derek. "Who wants to volunteer?"

An abrupt silence fell over the room. "Don't everybody rush forward at once," said Joe finally.

"Are *you* volunteering, Hardy?" asked Derek.

"Maybe I am," said Joe, pulling something out of his pocket. "Here. I broke that piece of plastic wire

50

off the spike ball and brought it with me. I thought it might come in handy. We can use it to pull open the door."

"Good thinking," said Frank.

"Thanks," said Joe, coiling the wire around the door handle. "First I tie this end of the wire around the handle of the door with the white keyhole—"

"I'll unlock the door," said Frank, taking the key from Derek and turning it in the lock.

"Now everybody get back into the last room," said Joe. There was a sudden rush as the rest of the group complied with Joe's request. "I just hope this wire is long enough to let me join you in there," said Joe, playing out the wire as he walked away from the door.

"*Just* long enough," said Frank, as Joe reached the door to the room they had just come out of.

"I also hope it doesn't break when I give it a tug," Joe added. "Everybody ready?"

"Ready as we'll ever be," said Frank. "Go ahead and open the door."

"Here goes," Joe said, yanking gently on the wire. The door didn't budge.

"Great," said Joe. "I'll have to pull harder."

He yanked again. The door still didn't move.

"Don't yank too hard," said Frank. "Remember that the wire was designed to break when somebody opened the door it was attached to. Pull it too hard and you might break it again."

"I *know* that," said Joe, "but I've got to get this door open. Cross your fingers."

Taking a deep breath, Joe gave the wire one last tug. Slowly at first, then more rapidly as he pulled harder, the door began to swing open.

"No sign of poison gas," said Frank. "We must have picked the right door."

"What if the gas is odorless?" suggested Win.

"And invisible," said Chet.

"Then we're all dead," said Joe. "Come on, don't start acting like wimps! You think the Secret Wizard Master's going to buy odorless, invisible gas at the neighborhood army surplus store? Get real!"

"I hate to say it," said Derek, "but Hardy's right. We don't have any choice but to go through that door. I'll go first, if none of the rest of you will."

"*I'll* go first," said Joe haughtily. "*I* opened the door."

"Fine with me if *everybody* goes first," said Chet. "Everybody except me."

Joe and Derek walked briskly across the room and through the door that Joe had just opened, each competing to be the first one through. "Well, I haven't dropped dead yet," said Joe. "And neither has Derek."

"Somebody had better find that poison gas canister," said Derek, "before it causes us any trouble."

"I don't see any poison gas canister," said Frank, looking around the room.

"Here's where the other door comes out," Pete said. "It leads into this room, too. If there was a canister of poison gas, this is where it would be. And it's not here."

"Then the Secret Wizard Master was bluffing," said Win. "There's no gas after all."

Joe bent over to pick up another roll of paper from the floor. "Here's another scroll," he said. He glanced at it briefly, then laughed. "Wait'll you hear this." He read:

"'SOME TRAPS ARE REAL.
SOME TRAPS ARE NOT.
IT'S NOT KNOWING WHICH
THAT THICKENS THE PLOT.'"

"So it *was* a bluff," said Frank.

"Pure and simple," agreed Pete. "This Secret Wizard Master is really playing us for fools."

"You've played worse tricks than that as Wizard Master, Pete," said Win.

"But that was a game!" said Pete angrily. "This is real. Our lives may be at stake. And this guy is toying with us!"

"Not much we can do about it," said Joe. "Let's take a look around this room and see where we are. Chet, hold the lantern up a little higher. I can't see."

"Yessir, Master Joe," said Chet, raising the lantern to shoulder height. "Right away, sir!"

"There's another one of those things on the wall," said Joe, pointing at an arrangement similar to one they had seen in an earlier room, with two long spears crossed beneath a brightly painted coat of arms.

In the center of the floor was a painted rug, like

53

the one that had earlier concealed the pit Joe had fallen into. Frank glared at it ominously.

"Watch out," he told the others. "There might be another mine shaft underneath it."

"Let's take a look," said Win. He pulled the rug aside, revealing a yawning hole underneath. "You're right! There's another pit."

The group stared down at the black hole in the center of the room. "The Secret Wizard Master's slipping," said Joe. "The same trick never works twice."

"He's just keeping us on our toes," said Derek. "This won't be the last trick he plays."

"There's another chest on the other side of the room," said Win. "Let's take a look in it."

"Be careful," said Pete. "He may have booby-trapped some of these chests, too."

"I'll be careful," said Win. He slowly unlatched the chest and raised the lid. "Hey, there's something in here that Chet will be glad to see!"

"Huh?" said Chet. "The only thing I'd be glad to see is—"

Win held up a parcel wrapped in plastic. "Chicken sandwiches, unless I miss my guess. Smells just like the kind my mother makes."

"I've died and gone to heaven!" cried Chet, racing heedlessly toward the sandwiches.

"Take it easy!" said Joe, grabbing Chet around his considerable waist. "You almost fell in the pit!"

"I'll float over it!" shouted Chet deliriously. "Just let me at those sandwiches!"

"Wait a minute!" said Frank urgently, grabbing

the sandwiches away from Win. "We don't know if this food is safe. There's a good chance that our friend the Secret Wizard Master has poisoned this food. And there's no way we can test it, not without eating it and risking our lives."

"I'll risk it!" said Chet, reaching out to take the sandwiches from Frank. "I'll be the official food tester! I'll eat all potentially poisoned food so that none of the rest of you have to risk your lives!"

"I can't let you do that," said Frank. "Here. I'll throw them away."

Frank tossed the parcel into the pit in the center of the room. Chet looked on in horror.

"Hey!" he shouted, belatedly trying to grab the sandwiches before they disappeared into the abyss. The lantern flew out of his hand and crashed to the ground next to the pit.

The light went out instantly. The room was plunged into total darkness!

"The lantern fell into the shaft!" moaned Pete. "Now we'll never find our way out of here!"

6 The Mad Orc's Lair

"We don't know that it fell into the hole," said Frank. "It might be on the floor somewhere."

"Broken into a thousand pieces, probably." Joe groaned. "Now we're trapped in the dark. Good work, Chet!"

"I can't believe you did that!" said Chet to Frank. "You threw away a package of chicken sandwiches! I don't care if they *were* poisoned!"

"I saw the lantern land right beside the shaft," said Derek. "Everybody stay real still, so the lantern doesn't get knocked into the hole."

"How will we find it if we don't move?" asked Win.

"Let me do it," said Derek. "I know where it is. I can find it by touch. Ah, I think I've got it—"

"Ouch!" shouted Joe. "That's my leg, you dip-stick!"

"Sorry. I think the lantern's right over here, next to . . . Here, I think this is it. I'm not grabbing anybody's leg, am I?"

"Just turn on the lantern and get this over with!" said Win. "I never noticed before, but I'm afraid of the dark."

"Right now we're *all* afraid of the dark!" said Frank.

"Uh-oh," said Derek. "I just threw the switch and the lantern didn't come on."

"I knew it!" said Pete. "It's broken! Chet probably smashed the bulb!"

"Don't blame me," said Chet. "Blame Frank. He's the one who threw the sandwiches in the pit!"

"Calm down," said Derek. "The bulb's okay. I think it's just . . ."

All of a sudden the light flashed on again, blindingly bright.

". . . just loose," said Derek, finishing the sentence. "There. I tightened it. Maybe I'll hang onto the lantern for a while, if nobody minds."

"Just so long as you don't give it to Chet again," said Pete angrily.

"Oh, great!" said Chet. "Make *me* the villain."

"Nobody's the villain," said Frank. "I'm sorry I had to throw away those sandwiches, Chet—"

"You didn't *have* to throw them away," snapped Chet.

"Break it up, boys!" said Derek. "Let's take a look around this room and decide what to do next."

57

"There aren't any more doors or chests," said Joe, "but it looks like there's a hole in the far wall. I wonder where it leads."

Derek held the lantern out at arm's length. Set into the far wall was a round hole, about three feet in diameter. Above the hole someone had taped a sign reading The Mad Orc's Lair.

"What's an orc?" Joe asked. "Sounds like the noise a seal makes. Orc! Orc!"

"It's an imaginary creature," said Win. "Sort of like a troll. We run into a lot of orcs in Wizards and Warriors. Most of them aren't very nice."

Derek thrust his lantern into the hole. Inside was a narrow passage extending deep into the wall, disappearing into dark shadows.

"It's a small tunnel leading farther into the mine," said Derek. "I can't see the end of it, but it appears to be the only direction we can go."

"There's always the third tunnel off the main room," said Pete.

"I think we should finish exploring this tunnel first," said Derek.

"Uh, listen," said Win to Frank. "Before we start exploring this tunnel, can I talk with you and Joe for a minute?"

"Sure," said Frank. "What about?"

"I'll tell you in a minute. I want this to be private, okay?"

Derek looked up. "Something you can't share with the rest of us, Win?" he asked.

"It's something I want to tell Frank and Joe. Alone."

"Well, if you don't trust me, Win . . ." Derek began.

"If one of you is the Secret Wizard Master," interrupted Frank, "maybe we *shouldn't* trust each other. Not too much, anyway." He turned back to Win. "We can talk in the other room, Win. Joe, come over here. Win has something to tell us."

The trio stepped back into the room they had come out of a few moments earlier. Only a few dim rays of light from the lantern seeped through the door.

"What is it, Win?" asked Joe. "Do you know something about the Secret Wizard Master that we don't?"

"I'm not sure," Win said. "Maybe. Everything that's happened here has seemed very familiar to me. Too familiar. When I saw that sign about the Mad Orc's Lair, I suddenly remembered why."

"Why?" asked Frank.

"Everything that's happened so far has been taken straight out of a new Wizards and Warriors scenario called *The Caves of Madness*. The Mad Orc's Lair, the spiked ball, the door with the poison behind it, even the pit that Joe fell into."

"That's interesting," said Frank.

"So whoever the Secret Wizard Master is," Joe said, "he must have read the scenario."

"Right," said Win. "And that's what's strange. You see, it hasn't been published yet."

"If it hasn't been published yet," asked Frank, "how do you know what's in it?"

"Pete got an advance copy from the publisher. He

told them about the paper he was writing on role-playing games, so they sent him a copy of the scenario . . . and he showed it to me."

"Did he show it to anybody else?" Joe asked. "Derek, for instance?"

"Not that I know of. You'll have to ask Pete."

"What else happens in this scenario?" asked Frank. "Maybe we should know a few details in advance, so we'll know what to expect from the Secret Wizard Master."

"I wish I could tell you," said Win, "but I really didn't get a chance to read it. I only skimmed it, and I don't remember everything. But Pete may have read it. You can ask him."

Frank looked at Joe. "Do you think Pete's the Secret Wizard Master? He's the group's *real* Wizard Master, after all . . . and he's the one who got an advance copy of the scenario."

"I don't know," said Joe. "I'm holding out for Derek being the Secret Wizard Master, just on general principles."

"Derek's obnoxious," said Frank, "but that doesn't necessarily mean he's trying to kill us."

"Well, maybe not," said Joe reluctantly. "But I don't trust him."

"I think we should talk to Pete about that scenario," said Frank. "Thanks for telling us about it, Win."

"I thought I should," said Win. "I've heard about the detective work you guys do. If anybody can catch the Secret Wizard Master and get us out of here, I think you're the ones."

"Thanks for the vote of confidence, Win," said Joe. "Now, let's go back and join the others."

They walked into the other room, where Derek was still peering into the narrow hole in the wall. Frank beckoned to Pete.

"Come over here for a second, Pete," he said. "Joe and I want to talk to you."

"Sure," said Pete. "What's up?"

"Win tells us that you got an advance copy of the next Wizards and Warriors scenario. Have you had a chance to read it yet?"

"Oh, yeah," Pete said. "*The Caves of Madness.* No, I haven't read it. Funny thing about that. It disappeared. I got it in the mail a couple of weeks ago and it vanished a couple of days later. I haven't seen it since."

"Then you never got to read it?"

"Not a single word. I don't even have any idea what it's about. Too bad. I was going to write about it in my paper."

"Okay, Pete, thanks," said Joe. "That's all we needed to know."

"Are you guys going to stand around chatting all day?" said Derek irritably. "I'm going into this hole. Who wants to join me?"

"I think Chet should go," said Pete, "to make up for dropping that lantern."

"That's not fair," said Chet. "I think Frank should go, to make up for throwing away those sandwiches."

"We'll *both* go," said Frank. "Does that sound fair?"

"I guess so," said Chet. "Who goes first?"

"After you, Chet," said Derek. "I'll come up behind you, carrying the lantern."

"I could carry the lantern," suggested Chet.

"Not on your life," said Derek.

"Oh, all right. But that tunnel isn't big enough for me to walk around in."

"It's not big enough for any of us to walk around in," said Frank. "You'll have to crawl in head first."

Chet shuddered. "Suppose there's something down there, like a bear?" he said. "I'd have to back out all the way, while it clawed my eyes out. No thank you. I'm going in feet first."

"Suit yourself," said Derek. "Then the bear can eat your toes off. Let's go."

Chet hesitated. "Uh, how am I going to get my feet into this hole?"

"Derek and I will give you a boost," said Frank, grabbing Chet's shoulder. "Just lean back and we'll shove you in."

"Okay," said Chet. "Here goes nothing."

"Oof," groaned Derek, as Chet leaned into his arms. "I'd say you're a little more than nothing, Morton. How much do you weigh, anyway?"

"That's a state secret," said Frank. "If the Russians found out, they'd build an army of Chet Mortons and eat the rest of the world into submission."

"Okay," said Chet, as Frank and Derek helped him into the tunnel. "I've got my feet in the hole. Just give me a push."

"We *are* pushing," said Frank.

"I feel like I'm pushing a tank," said Derek. "Are you moving at all, Morton?"

62

"Yeah," said Chet. "I'm just about inside the hole. Okay, I can move on my own now. Better get that lantern in here, though. It's awfully dark."

Derek poked his head into the hole after Chet. "Okay," he said. "I'll be right behind you, Chet. Just keep moving."

"Hurry back, you guys," said Joe, standing beside the hole. "It'll be awfully dark up here without the lantern."

"Want to join us?" said Frank.

"No, thanks," said Joe. "Four's a crowd in a hole that small. Just come back and tell us what you find."

The room was almost completely dark as Derek and Chet crawled away down the narrow tunnel. Frank squirmed into the hole after the others. The narrow passage inside the hole wasn't as cramped as Frank had expected. There was room for his shoulders, and his head didn't scrape the ceiling, though there wasn't enough room for him to stand up. Ahead of him, he could see the flicker of Derek's lantern, but most of the light was blocked by Derek's body.

"You two okay?" he shouted.

"Couldn't be better," said Derek unenthusiastically.

"Pretty dark up here," said Chet. "I can't even see where I'm going."

"Your knees are in the way," Derek pointed out.

"Well, yeah," said Chet. "But it's still pretty dark."

"Can you see where the tunnel goes?" asked Frank.

"No way," said Chet. "And it makes me nervous. I don't know if I'm about to fall into a shaft or something."

"Just go slow," said Frank.

"He's already going slow enough," said Derek. "We're never going to get the place explored at this rate."

"Hey!" shouted Chet with sudden urgency. "Something just touched my ankles!"

"What do you mean?" said Derek. "Did you bump into something?"

"No!" shouted Chet, his voice shaking with fear. "It . . . it feels like something . . . alive!"

"Alive?" asked Frank. "Chet, have you gone completely bonkers?"

"He-e-e-e-e-e-e-elp!" cried Chet at the top of his lungs. "Something's grabbed me by the legs! It's pulling on me! Get me outta here!"

"What's happening, Derek?" shouted Frank. "Can you see anything?"

"All I can see is the top of Chet's head!" replied Derek. "But he's moving! Fast! Like something's pulling him!"

"Somebody do something!" shouted Chet. "It's got me! He-e-e-e-e-lp!"

"Grab him, Derek!" shouted Frank. "Do something!"

"I'm trying!" Derek responded, crawling forward as rapidly as his arms and legs would take him. "He's moving too quickly! I can't get hold of him!"

"No-o-o-o-o-o!" cried Chet's voice, receding into

the distant recesses of the tunnel. "Somebody help me-e-e-e-e-e-e——!"

Chet's voice seemed to trail off into silence, as Frank and Derek scrambled down the tunnel after him. The lantern in Derek's hand bobbed wildly, sending strange patterns of light and shadow shooting up and down the narrow walls.

Finally Derek came to a halt and paused for a moment to listen for sounds of Chet in the darkness. "There's no sign of him," Derek said at last. "I don't know what happened to him. I think he's gone!"

7 Duel to the Death

"What do you mean, gone?" asked Frank. "He can't be gone!"

"I meant what I said," snapped Derek. "He's gone! I can't see or hear him. He's vanished."

"Keep moving," said Frank. "He's got to be up ahead someplace."

"Okay, we'll keep looking," said Derek. "But I don't think we're going to find anything."

Far behind them, Frank and Derek could hear shouting from the room where the others were waiting. The voices were too far away to understand, so they ignored them, concentrating instead on finding Chet.

"I see something up ahead," said Derek.

"What is it?" asked Frank.

"I can't make it out yet. It looks like something

painted silver. It's . . . I think it's Chet's helmet and sword."

"Any sign of Chet?"

"No," said Derek. "Just the helmet and sword."

"Keep going, then," said Frank.

"I can't. There's a wall up ahead."

Frank shivered. "A wall? How can that be? Where's Chet?"

"There's a mine shaft here, too, but there's no ladder inside. In fact, I can't see anything at all inside it."

"Could Chet have fallen into the shaft?" asked Frank.

"How in the world am I supposed to know?" snapped Derek. "Maybe he was eaten by a bear."

"Very funny! Something terrible may have happened to Chet and you're making jokes!"

Derek sighed. "I'm sorry. I don't know what's happened to Chet. I do know that there's nothing we can do. Without a ladder, we can't go down the mine shaft."

"I guess you're right," said Frank finally. "We'd better get out of here."

"Can you turn around?" asked Derek.

"I think so," said Frank, awkwardly reorienting himself in the tunnel. "Okay, I'm facing the other way."

"You're in the lead now," said Derek. "I'll bring up the rear with the lantern. I hope whatever got Chet doesn't come up behind me."

"You and me both," said Frank.

It took five minutes for Frank and Derek to make their way back to the tunnel entrance. When they got there, the others were gathered around the entrance waiting for them, everyone talking at once.

"What happened?" asked Pete.

"We heard screaming!" said Win.

"Where's Chet?" asked Joe.

"We don't know where Chet is," said Derek.

"Something got him," said Frank bitterly. "He said that something was dragging him by the ankles, and then he was gone. This is all that was left." He held out Chet's helmet and sword.

"What do you mean, something got him?" shouted Joe. "How could something get Chet? This is terrible!"

Win's eyes opened wide. "The mad orc!" he said breathlessly.

"Calm down, Win," said Pete. "There's no such thing as an orc."

"The sign said that this was the mad orc's lair," said Win. "And something got Chet down there!"

"I think *I* know what got Chet!" said Joe angrily. "I saw Derek go into the tunnel right after Chet! He must have been the last one to see Chet alive!"

"Are you implying something, Hardy?" asked Derek.

"You bet I am!" snapped Joe. "Could you see what happened down there, Frank? Or are you just taking Derek's word for it?"

"Joe," said Frank, "I'm as upset about what happened to Chet as you are, but that's no reason to

68

blame Derek for it. I couldn't see what happened in the tunnel, but that doesn't mean——"

"I think it means that Derek had something to do with what happened to Chet!" interrupted Joe. "I don't know how you did it, Derek, but I think you know where Chet is now!"

"He couldn't have had anything to do with it!" said Frank. "I heard Chet yelling that something had him by the ankles. There's no way that Derek could have grabbed Chet by the ankles. He was *behind* Chet."

"Maybe he had accomplices," said Joe. "I think Derek set Chet up for a trap."

"That's enough, Hardy!" said Derek ominously. "I'm not going to let you stand there and say things like that about me!"

"What are you going to do about it?" said Joe.

"This!" said Derek, pulling his sword from the belt around his waist. "Win, give Joe your sword! We're going to have a duel!"

"Uh, I don't think that's such a good idea," said Win hesitantly.

"I think it's a lousy idea," said Frank.

"Well, I think it's a great idea," said Joe, grabbing the sword away from Win. "Come on, Hannon. I've been wanting to take a poke at you all day! I'd prefer fists, but if you want swords, we'll use swords!"

"My pleasure," said Derek, pointing his sword ominously in Joe's direction. "Here, Win. You hold the lantern!"

"Cut it out, you two!" shouted Frank. "Those

swords may be made out of wood, but you could still hurt yourselves with them, and that wouldn't help anything."

"Stay out of this, Frank!" said Joe. "Derek's been asking for this all along. It's time we got it over with. Besides, I'm not going to hurt him. Just teach him a lesson."

"That's right, Frank," said Derek. "Stay out of this. This is between me and your brother. Maybe we'll settle this once and for all."

Almost before he had finished speaking, Derek lunged forward with his sword. Joe, startled by the speed of Derek's movement, barely ducked aside in time. He quickly brought up his sword and tried to hit Derek over the head with the flat side of it, but Derek moved out of the way as quickly as he had lunged.

"Too quick for you, Hardy?" asked Derek with a sneer.

Joe gulped. "N-nothing of the sort, Derek. You're lucky I didn't finish you off right there!"

"I suppose I am!" said Derek with an arrogant laugh. "I guess I'll have to give you another chance!"

Derek lunged at Joe again. This time Joe managed to get his sword into position in time to deflect Derek's sword to one side. Derek pulled his sword back and smiled.

"Pretty good, Hardy," he said. "You might make a decent sword fighter yet. Pity you weren't born four hundred years ago."

"Pity *you* weren't," said Joe. "Then we wouldn't have to put up with you anymore."

70

"You'd love to get rid of me, wouldn't you, Hardy? Because you're scared of me, right? Because you know I'm better at everything than you are!"

Joe's eyes flashed with rage. "You conceited bag of wind! I ought to—" He lunged forward wildly with his sword, aiming it straight at Derek. But the other boy simply stepped aside with a grin, barely troubling to avoid Joe's wildly aimed thrust.

"Nice try, Hardy, but no cigar," said Derek. "You've got to learn to control the sword."

"I'll control *you!*" shouted Joe, turning and lunging once again at Derek.

"Hah!" shouted Derek, moving his sword upward rapidly and catching Joe's sword at the hilt. The sword popped right out of Joe's hand and flew through the air, landing several feet away.

"What the—?" Joe stared after the sword in astonishment.

"Guess I won that match, eh, Hardy?" sneered Derek.

"Not on your life!" shouted Joe. He reached up to the wall and grabbed one of the spears displayed underneath the coat of arms. "I'm not out of this duel as long as I've got a weapon!" He raised the spear and pointed it at Derek. It was about twice as long as Derek's sword and sharply pointed.

"That won't be much longer," said Derek casually. He swung his sword at Joe's spear, neatly breaking it in two.

Joe looked down at his mutilated spear. He was holding one end of a curtain rod. "A fake!" he muttered. "I should have known."

71

"I think this foolishness has gone on long enough," said Derek. "Surrender or pay the price, Hardy!"

"I'll never surrender to you, Hannon," said Joe nervously, backing away from Derek's outthrust sword. Out of the corner of his eye Joe could see the sword that Derek had knocked out of his hand. If only he could reach it.

Suddenly Joe's foot touched the gaping hole in the center of the room. He swiveled to one side to avoid falling into the pit and lost his balance, tumbling instead to the floor of the room.

"This is it!" cried Derek, leaping to Joe's side and placing a foot on his chest. As Joe looked up in horror, Derek placed the end of the sword against Joe's Adam's apple. "I'm going to finish you off for good, Hardy!"

8 The Third Tunnel

Frank and Pete grabbed Derek and pulled him away from Joe. Derek stumbled backward, dropping his sword, a dazed look coming over his face.

"I . . . I'm sorry," he stammered suddenly. "I don't know what came over me. I . . . I guess I got a little carried away."

"A little carried away?" said Frank. "You almost killed my brother!"

"No," said Derek, honest remorse in his voice. "I wasn't really going to hurt him. I just wanted to teach him a lesson, scare him a little."

Win helped Joe back to his feet. "Scare me?" said Joe. "You were going to kill me! You had that sword at my throat! You could have crushed my windpipe."

Derek shook his head. The confidence was gone from his face and his voice was beginning to tremble.

"That was stupid of me. I just got caught up in the sword fight. I wanted to prove I could outfight you."

"Well, you did," said Joe reluctantly. "You're a better sword fighter than I am, even if you're a lousy human being."

"I guess I deserved that," said Derek. "You have my apologies, Joe, for what that's worth."

"That and a handful of quarters will buy me a soda," said Joe sullenly.

"Listen," said Pete. "I hate to interrupt this, but I think we'd better get back to finding our way out of here. The batteries in that lantern aren't going to last all night."

"You're right, Pete," said Frank. "And the quicker we get out, the sooner we can find out what's happened to Chet. Come on, Joe. You and Derek can talk this out later."

"We don't have anything to talk about," said Joe. "Here's your sword, Win. Try not to get in any sword fights."

"Where to next?" said Pete. "We seem to be at the end of this tunnel. Do we head back and check out the third tunnel?"

"What else?" said Win. "Maybe it leads to the exit."

"Then let's go," said Frank. Once again, the group trudged back toward the first room. As they walked in a weary procession, Win appeared at Frank and Joe's shoulders.

"I remembered a little more about that *Caves of Madness* scenario. I don't know if it's important or not, but . . ."

"You might as well tell us about it," said Frank. "You never know what might be relevant."

"Okay," said Win. "The object of the scenario was to find the Treasure of the Dwarven King."

"The Treasure of the Dwarven King?" echoed Joe.

"Yeah," said Win. "I think that was some kind of stash of gold and jewels that was at the bottom of the Caves of Madness. The goal of the game was to get to the bottom of the caves and find the treasure."

"Which is sort of what we're doing, right?" said Frank.

"Right!" said Win, with a quick smile.

"So what's the treasure?" asked Joe. "The exit? Or something else?"

"I don't know," said Win. "I can't wait to find out!"

Frank looked Win in the eye. "You're actually enjoying this, aren't you? You think this is fun."

Win's face fell. "Of . . . of course not!" he said. "Why would I be enjoying this? Chet's missing and our lives are in danger!"

"Frank's right," said Joe. "You think this is a big game, don't you? Is your life really that dull, Win?"

Win shrugged. "I don't know. Yeah, I guess you're right. Maybe I am enjoying this. If I wasn't trapped in this cave, I'd be working at Bergmeyer's or doing homework for math class. I think I'd rather be in this cave. Is that a crime?"

"No," said Frank. "It's not a crime. It's just a pity."

"Yeah," said Joe. "Maybe you should get out more, Win. Stop playing so many games. Start living a life."

75

"You guys are popular," said Win. "I'm not. Games are all I have."

"Maybe you just haven't tried," said Frank. "Join some clubs at school. Make some friends."

"Listen," said Joe. "After we get out of here, Frank and I'll take you to Mr. Pizza, introduce you to a few of our friends. Maybe you'll get along with them."

Anger flashed in Win's eyes. "You have no right to tell me what's wrong with my life. I happen to *like* my life. I like playing games." He turned and stormed away.

"Wait a minute," said Joe. "That's not what I meant! I . . . "

"Relax, Joe," said Frank. "If Win wants to get angry over that, let him get angry. You did get a little rough on him."

"I guess you're right," said Joe. "This whole Dungeon of Doom thing is starting to get to me. I got carried away. I'll apologize to him later."

The group marched wearily into the main room. There was one door left that they had not yet entered. The keyhole was painted a bright blue.

"I've got the key," said Win, holding it up where the others could see. "Ready to enter?"

"Be careful, Win," said Pete. "Remember that spiked ball that you almost walked into earlier."

"I'll be careful," said Win, turning the key in the lock. "Everybody stand back while I open the door."

He pulled the door open slowly. When nothing happened, Derek held up the lantern so that they could see into the next room.

"I think it's safe," Derek said.

"Follow me," said Win, stepping through the door.

The room was nearly bare, except for another chest. Pete opened it. There was another battery inside.

"Thank goodness," said Derek. "I put the second battery in about a half hour ago. I don't know how much longer it's going to last."

"Let's hope we don't get the chance to find out," said Frank. "Maybe the exit isn't too far away now."

"Maybe," said Pete. "The next door looks like it shouldn't be any problem."

Frank followed Pete's gaze to the far wall. There was a single, door-size opening in the wall, with no door blocking the way.

"At least we don't have to worry about a key," said Frank, walking to the doorway. He began to step inside.

Suddenly Joe, who was standing directly behind him, cried out, "Stop, Frank! Don't move any farther!"

Frank froze in his tracks. "What is it?" he said. "What's wrong?"

"Look in the room," said Joe, pointing over Frank's shoulder. "On the floor!"

Frank did as Joe suggested. Propped on the floor of the next room was a large wooden crossbow, with the string pulled taut and held fast by a curved wooden stick bolted to the floor. Attached to the stick and holding it in place was a wire, which ran straight to the doorway, where it passed through a

pair of loops that suspended it directly across the passageway, forming a trip wire.

Frank's leg was pressed against the trip wire. If he moved his leg either forward or backward, there was a good chance that he would jiggle the trip wire and release the string.

Balanced delicately between the bow and the string was a hefty metal arrow, with a formidable looking point.

And it was aimed directly at Frank's chest!

9 Crossing the Abyss

"Just stand still!" said Joe urgently. "Don't move!"

"You don't have to tell me twice!" said Frank. "I won't even breathe!"

"Lean over so I can get in there and disarm the crossbow," said Joe. "You're blocking the doorway."

"I can't lean any farther," said Frank. "I'm up against the edge of the doorway already. And if I move, I might trigger the crossbow."

"There's no space for me to get around you," said Joe. "What am I supposed to do?"

"Go over his shoulder," said Derek. "Here. I'll give you a boost."

"Get lost, Hannon," said Joe. "I don't want your help! Not after you tried to crush my Adam's apple."

"Take his help!" shouted Frank desperately. "There's an arrow aimed at my chest!"

Joe gave Derek a nasty look. "All right, Hannon, but make it fast. That bow might go off any second."

"No sooner said than done," said Derek, kneeling behind Joe and lacing his hands on the floor. "Put one foot in my hands and the other against the wall. Get a good grip on Frank's shoulder and I'll give you a push. Then climb over Frank's shoulder and into the next room."

"Take it easy," said Frank. "Don't shake my leg. That string looks like it's going to snap any second."

"Okay," said Joe, reluctantly following Derek's instructions. "I'm ready to go. Give me a lift."

With a grunt, Derek pulled up on Joe's leg. Frank winced as Joe pressed down on his shoulder with his hands, then threw his other leg next to Frank's neck.

"Whew!" shouted Frank. "You must weigh as much as Chet! Hurry up before I collapse on top of the bow!"

"Don't rush me," said Joe. "I don't want to land on the trip wire. I might cause the bow to fire." He surveyed the floor on the other side of Frank. "All right, I'm going to jump."

"It can't happen too soon," said Frank. "Derek, give him a push."

"Here you go, Joe," said Derek. "Get your other leg over. That's right. Now jump!"

Joe jumped, landing inches from the crossbow. Gingerly, he turned around and surveyed the situation. The bow was still taut and the trip wire was vibrating slightly from the impact of his leap.

"Now what?" said Joe. "I can't cut the wire, or the arrow will fire."

"Grab the arrow!" said Frank. "Pull it out of the bow before it can fire!"

"No!" said Derek. "Put your leg in between the string and the bow! That way, even if the string is released, the arrow won't fire!"

Joe heeded the advice. "Okay, now I'm going to get the arrow," he said, slowly bending down toward the bow.

Even as he touched the arrow, the string snapped loose from the stick that was holding it in place and wrapped itself around Joe's leg. The arrow popped limply from the bow and landed at Frank's feet.

Frank sagged at the knees. "I think I'm ready to take a break," he said.

"Aren't we all?" said Derek.

Joe looked around the room he had just entered. Derek held up the lantern to illuminate the walls, as the others filed in.

"Nothing in here," Joe said. "Not even any doors. Another dead end."

"Terrific," Pete said. "This was the last passage. Where do we go now?"

"There was that door we couldn't get through in the first passage," suggested Win.

"Right," said Frank. "The one with the purple keyhole. Has anyone seen a purple key?"

"Not yet," said Derek. "And there don't seem to be any more chests."

"I guess we'd better go back to the purple door, then," said Win.

"What good will that do?" Joe said. "We don't have a key."

"Maybe we'll think of something when we get there," said Frank. "Come on. Have you got a better idea?"

"Not really," said Joe. "I wish I did."

"Then it's back to the front room again," said Pete.

"I know the route in my sleep," said Win.

Minutes later, they regrouped at the right-hand door leading out of the first room. The door was still open, as they had left it earlier.

"Everybody, be careful," said Derek. "Remember the pit in the first room."

"We'll be careful," said Frank, leading the way through the door. Minutes later, they were standing in front of the door with the purple keyhole.

"Still no purple key," said Frank. "Anybody have any ideas about how to open it?"

"We could try battering it open," said Joe.

"This door is strong," Pete said. "But if you want to bruise your shoulder on it, be my guest."

"Well," said Frank, "I vote that we take a breather until somebody comes up with a bright idea. Why don't we all sit down?"

"Sounds good," said Win. "My feet are getting sore."

"Mine, too," said Pete, settling to the floor. "I should have worn softer shoes."

"Guess you didn't expect to be doing so much walking this evening," said Joe, sitting next to Frank.

Derek crouched next to Joe, who flashed him a dirty look. "Listen, Joe," said Derek. "I really do want to apologize for what happened earlier. I had no right to do the things I did."

Joe stared at the wall for a moment, refusing to meet Derek's gaze. "All right," he said finally. "I guess I'm sort of to blame, too. I goaded you into that duel. Maybe I needed to be taught a lesson."

"Don't worry about that," said Derek. "I want to make it up to you. How about a sword fighting lesson?"

Joe looked at Derek suspiciously. "What are you talking about?"

"You did better than I expected in that fight. Your technique is a little rough, but you've got some pretty slick moves. I could give you a few pointers. You never know when they'll come in handy."

"Right!" Joe laughed. "Just last week I had to turn down a sword fight because I hadn't had any lessons yet."

"Don't laugh," said Derek. "These swords are the only weapons we've got and we might need them before we get out of this place. When you meet the Secret Wizard Master face-to-face, you might need more than your wits and your fists."

Joe thought about it for a minute. "Well, you may have a point. Okay, I guess we've got a little time. What do you want to show me?"

Derek stood up, pulled out his sword, and extended it at arm's length. "Just do as I do," he said. "I think you'll pick up the technique."

"I don't have a sword," said Joe.

"Oh, right. Win, can you lend Joe your sword again?"

The others turned toward Derek and Joe. "Are you two dueling again?" asked Win.

"I thought you'd learned your lesson after the last time," added Frank, a concerned frown on his face.

"No, no," said Derek. "I'm just showing Joe how to use a sword. He can't use Chet's—it's made of rubber. I thought you could lend him yours, Win."

Win looked at Joe. "Well, if you're sure you're not going to tear into each other again."

"Not this time," said Joe, extending his hand. Win handed him the sword. "Thanks, Win. Now what, Derek?"

"Hold the sword like this," said Derek. "And keep your elbow bent like this."

Joe did as Derek instructed. "And then what do I do?"

"If you should find yourself threatened by somebody else with a sword, the first thing you should do is . . ."

For the next fifteen minutes, while the others talked about ways to get through the door with the purple lock, Joe and Derek fought a mock duel, with Derek giving Joe pointers on what he was doing wrong. Finally, Derek put down his sword and clapped Joe on the back.

"You're pretty good," he said. "You're naturally athletic. You've got the strength to lift a heavy sword and a good sense of timing. There's another thing I want to show you. Then I think you'll be able to hold

your own in a fight against an inexperienced opponent."

"What about an experienced opponent?" asked Joe.

"You're not *that* good," said Derek. "Sword fighting takes a lot of practice. All I've shown you are the basics."

"What was the last thing you wanted to show me?"

"The Sicilian Switchback," said Derek with a smile.

"The what?" asked Joe in a baffled tone.

"It's a little-known sword fighting technique, almost guaranteed to catch your opponent off guard. I used it on you earlier, when I knocked the sword out of your hand."

"How does it work?" asked Joe.

"It's simple. I'll show you. Thrust at me with your sword, like you would in a regular fight."

"Well, okay," said Joe. He held the sword out in front of him the way Derek had shown him and lunged forward. Derek's sword moved up and down in a kind of W-shaped motion. Joe automatically moved his own sword to compensate for Derek's movement. All at once Derek's sword was at Joe's wrist, catching the handle of Joe's sword and ripping it from his hand.

"Hey!" said Joe. "How did you do that?"

"Try it yourself," said Derek. "The trick is in the W motion. You've got to do it at just the right second. Here. I'll thrust at you and you do it to me."

"I'll try," said Joe, picking up the sword. "I can't guarantee it'll work."

"Just hold your sword at an angle, like I did," said Derek. "Now, as I come at you"—Derek began to lunge—"bring the sword up, then down, then up again. That's it."

Joe's sword banged against the handle of Derek's but didn't knock it out of his hand. "You've got to bring it up faster," said Derek. "Put all the strength of your arm behind it."

They repeated the maneuver. This time Joe caught the handle of Derek's sword and nearly pulled the sword out of his hand.

"You've almost got it," said Derek. "Let's try again."

Derek lunged at Joe one more time. Joe moved his sword rapidly up and down—and knocked Derek's sword halfway across the room.

"Yeah!" said Derek. "That's the way to do it!"

"Hey!" said Joe. "Maybe I do know what I'm doing!"

"That'll be the day," said Frank, who had glanced up at the sound of Derek's sword hitting the floor. "Why don't you two save the sword fighting lessons for later and help us figure out how to get through this door?"

"Sure," said Derek, picking up his sword from where it had landed.

"Uh, has anybody actually tried to *open* the door?" asked Joe as he handed Win's sword back to him.

The others stared at one another for a moment.

86

"Well, no," said Pete. "We just assumed it was locked, like all the other doors. It's got a painted keyhole, after all."

"It never hurts to try," said Joe, walking to the door. He turned the handle and pulled. The door popped open effortlessly.

"I can't believe this!" said Frank. "We've been sitting here for fifteen minutes and the door isn't even locked!"

Joe leaned against the door and held his arm out in a beckoning gesture, motioning the others into the next room. Derek filed through first, holding the lantern. Pete and Win followed. Finally Frank walked to the door and paused for a moment.

"We'll be with you guys in a minute," he called after the others. "Joe and I have to talk."

Joe looked at Frank quizzically. "What about?" he asked.

"About this Secret Wizard Master business," said Frank. "Before we go any further into this . . . this dungeon, I think we'd better compare notes."

"I don't have any notes worth comparing," said Joe. "You know everything I do."

"You must have a hunch," said Frank. "We should be able to figure out who this Secret Wizard Master is by now." He frowned. "Especially since we've probably been in the same room with him for the last couple of hours."

"True," said Joe. "Well, we can always try the process of elimination. Let's run down the list, starting with the ones that we're sure *aren't* the Secret Wizard Master."

"I guess the two of us are at the top of that list," said Frank.

"Right," said Joe. "I'm sure that *I'm* not the Secret Wizard Master. And I'm *pretty* sure that you're not."

"I appreciate that leap of faith," Frank responded dryly. "We can also be pretty sure that Chet, wherever he is, is not the Secret Wizard Master."

"I'll buy that," said Joe. "And that only leaves three people."

"Derek, Pete, and Win," said Frank.

"So which one do you think it is?" asked Joe.

"I don't know. But I'm suspicious of the way Derek has suddenly started acting."

Joe gave Frank an affronted look. "Derek? Hey, he's all right. He just feels bad about that sword fight earlier."

Frank cocked an eyebrow. "I never expected to hear *you* say that. An hour ago he was at your throat."

"Well . . ." said Joe hesitantly, "maybe I was wrong about him."

"All right," said Frank. "We'll leave Derek aside for the moment. What about Pete?"

Joe thought about it. "I'm not sure. He did have the advance copy of *The Caves of Madness* scenario, but he claims he didn't read it. He's the only one besides Win who had a chance to see it before it disappeared."

"Do you think somebody stole the scenario?" asked Frank.

"Maybe," Joe said, nodding. "But if so, there's no telling who took it. We don't even know if Pete's

telling the truth when he says it vanished. If he's the Secret Wizard Master, he wouldn't want us to know he'd read the scenario."

"That leaves Win. Do you think he could be the Secret Wizard Master?"

"I don't know. He doesn't seem like the type. Too wrapped up in his imagination to have much to do with the real world."

"Yeah," said Frank. "I can't quite figure Win out. I'm not sure if he hasn't decided what to do with his life yet, or if he really does want to spend it playing games."

"Hey, you guys," Pete shouted from the next room. "I hate to interrupt, but you'd better take a look at this."

"Be right there," said Frank. He turned back to Joe. "We'll talk more about this later, okay?"

"Okay," said Joe. "Now we'd better see what Pete's yelling about."

The next room was large and decorated with the by-now-familiar coat of arms on the wall. The rest of the group had gathered toward the far end of the room. Derek was holding his lantern out, examining something that Frank and Joe couldn't see.

"What's the problem?" asked Frank. "Have we run out of doors again?"

"Worse," said Win. "Take a look at this."

Just beyond where the group was standing a gaping abyss cut across the floor of the mine. It was about eight feet across, too wide to risk jumping over. Frank and Joe looked over the edge, but they could not see the bottom.

"Terrific," said Joe. "Where'd this come from?"

"That doesn't matter. Got any ideas how we can cross it?" said Frank.

"Yes," said Derek. "Our invisible opponent has left us a means of transportation . . . right there!"

He pointed to a spot directly over the center of the abyss. Dangling above the darkness was a thick rope, anchored to the ceiling by a metal hook. It swayed slightly in the air.

"That's real useful," said Joe. "How do we reach it?"

"With one of these," said Frank. He reached up to the nearest wall and pulled down one of the phony spears from the coat-of-arms display. Popping the imitation spear point off one end of the old curtain rod, he bent the thin metal of the rod into a hook.

"It should just reach," said Frank, sticking the rod out over the abyss and snagging the rope with the hook. After three tries, Frank had the end of the rope in his hand.

"Now what, Tarzan?" asked Joe. "Are you going to swing across?"

"You have a better idea?" Frank asked. "If there's an exit from this place, it must be on the other side of this little canyon. If you'd like to stay over here, be my guest."

"No thanks," said Joe. "But you can go first."

"Aunt Gertrude would be proud of your manners," Frank said, handing the makeshift hook to his brother. "Here goes."

Frank gripped the rope tightly with both hands and leapt into the air, pushing against the edge of

the abyss with his feet. For an instant he seemed to hang suspended in space, then his feet caught the far side of the abyss and he let go of the rope.

"Whew!" he said, wobbling unsteadily on his feet. "I'm glad the Secret Wizard Master uses good, strong rope. Anybody like to join me?"

"I'm on my way," said Joe, using the hook to draw the rope back to his side of the canyon, then handing the hook to Derek. He grabbed the rope and leapt. "Geronimo!" he shouted loudly.

Derek followed, the lantern in one hand and the rope in the other. Then Pete swung across. Finally Win hooked the rope, took it in hand, then tossed the hook across to the others. "We'll need that if we have to come back across," he said.

"Good thinking," said Frank.

Win gripped the rope and gave it a mild tug. "I hope this rope holds for one more swing across the canyon," he said.

"It should," said Frank. "It felt pretty strong to me. Anyway, what choice do you have?"

"None, I guess," said Win. He grabbed the rope and began his leap.

Then, when he was halfway across to the other side, there was a groaning sound from the upper part of the room. The hook that the rope hung from popped out of the ceiling, sending Win plummeting toward the abyss!

10 Deeper and Deeper

Thud!

Win struck the ledge on the far side of the abyss with his arms and chest. Joe and Frank pounced on his arms, grabbing them tightly so that he wouldn't fall into the depths below.

"Ow!" cried Win, closing his eyes in pain. "You're crushing my hands!"

"You'll hurt more than your hands if you fall into that hole," said Joe.

Win opened his eyes and looked down. His face turned pale.

"Scratch what I just said," Win muttered. "Thanks for crushing my hands."

"You're welcome," said Frank. He and his brother

pulled Win out of the abyss and back up to solid ground.

"So much for turning back," said Derek. "That rope was the only way across. We'd better hope that this is the route to the exit, because we'll never get across that abyss again."

"Where else could the exit be?" Pete asked. "We've looked everywhere."

"I guess so," said Derek. "Are you okay, Win?"

"More or less," Win replied. "Like Joe said earlier, I'm just a little shook-up."

"I don't mean to shake everybody else up," said Joe, "but it looks like we've got another problem."

"Uh-oh," said Frank. "What now?"

"There's no door out of this room," Joe said ominously.

"What?" cried Derek. "After risking our lives crossing the abyss, we're at a dead end?"

"Looks that way," said Win.

Derek held up the lantern to illuminate the far end of the room. As Joe had said, there were no doors, only a blank expanse of grayish brown wall.

"What a mess!" said Joe. "An abyss on one side of us, a wall on the other. And we thought we were trapped before!"

Frank held up his hands. "I think it's time we had a reckoning here."

"A reckoning?" asked Win, a puzzled look on his face.

"We're agreed that the Secret Wizard Master is one of us, right?" Frank asked.

"Pretty much," said Pete. "What about it?"

"That means the Secret Wizard Master is trapped on this ledge, too," said Frank. "Without food, and without additional batteries for the lantern. My bet is that he doesn't plan to starve to death in darkness just to keep his identity a secret. So I'm asking here and now that the Secret Wizard Master speak up and help us get out of here. You'll be saving your own life, too, whoever you are."

A hush fell over the room. The members of the group stared at one another questioningly, but no one spoke.

Finally Frank broke the silence. "Are you the Secret Wizard Master, Pete? You're the group's real Wizard Master. Did you get tired of just playing the game in your imagination?"

Pete looked appalled. "Frank, nothing could be further from the truth. Wizards and Warriors is just a game to me, that's all. It's something I do a couple of days a week. My college studies are far more impor- tant to me. I'd much rather be studying for my next psychology exam than wandering around in this old mine."

Frank nodded. "Okay, Pete. I'll have to assume that that's true. But if it turns out not to be, I'll remember that you didn't help us when we needed the help. And I suspect the others will remember, too."

"I'd love to help us get out of here," said Pete. "But I can't. I don't know anything more than the rest of you do."

"What about you, Win?" asked Frank. "Are you the Secret Wizard Master?"

Win shook his head. "I almost wish I could say I was, but I can't. I like Wizards and Warriors a lot, but not so much that I'd allow myself to be trapped on this ledge for the chance to play it."

"You saw *The Caves of Madness* scenario," Joe reminded him. "You knew about the Lair of the Mad Orc and the Treasure of the Dwarven King."

"What are you guys talking about?" asked Derek. "I've never heard of a scenario called *The Caves of Madness.*"

"It's due to come out next month," said Frank. "Win told us about it earlier."

"But anyone else could have seen it, too," Win pointed out. "Pete told you that it's missing. Anyone could have taken it."

"True," said Frank. "What about you, Derek? Did you take it? Are you the Secret Wizard Master?"

"No," said Derek firmly. "I don't want to be in this place any more than the rest of you. I was supposed to be at football practice this evening, after which I was going to study physics and calculus."

"A little light reading?" asked Joe, with a smile.

"You could say that," Derek replied. "And I've never seen the scenario for *The Caves of Madness.* I'm not even sure what it has to do with all of this."

"Win thinks that the situation we're in bears a striking resemblance to the scenario," explained Frank. "Apparently the Lair of the Mad Orc is in it and a few other things."

"Including the Crossing of the Bottomless Abyss," said Win, nodding at the canyon they had just crossed.

"What happens *after* the crossing of the abyss?" asked Joe.

"I wish I could tell you," said Win. "Like I said, I only skimmed it."

"You sure remembered a lot of details," said Derek, giving him a hard look.

"It was only a scenario," replied Win defensively. "It tells you how to get into a situation, not necessarily how to get out of it. Besides, we don't know that the Secret Wizard Master is following the scenario exactly."

"So far he seems to have followed it pretty closely," said Frank. "And it looks like he's not willing to admit to his identity. I guess we'll have to think our way out of this situation."

Joe smiled. "Well, it's lucky we've got my brainpower to call on in this situation. Unfortunately, my brain hasn't come up with anything yet."

"What about the rest of you?" Frank asked. "You've played plenty of games of Wizards and Warriors in this dungeon. Did you ever get back to this room? Do you remember anything about it that could help us out?"

"I'm not sure," said Win, "but I think I once did get back this far into the mine. I seem to recall that this room was shaped a little differently than it is now. The rear wall was farther back from the abyss and the floor sloped downward. It looks more level now than I recall it looking." He looked around.

"The floor did go downhill—for quite a distance," he added. "And there was no wall there." Win pointed to the rear wall of the room.

Frank's eyes widened. "No wall? How could the Secret Wizard Master have built a new wall?"

"The light's dim in here," said Joe, walking toward the wall. "Maybe it's not a real wall at all."

"How does it look close up?"

"As phony as a three-dollar bill," said Joe, putting out his hand to touch the wall. "And it feels like papier-mâché. This wall is made out of construction paper and tissues."

"What about the floor?" asked Frank. "If the floor in this room slopes downward, what are we standing on?"

"Some kind of platform?" suggested Pete.

"Sure," said Joe. "A wooden platform. Stomp your feet."

Several members of the group did so. A hollow sound echoed through the room.

Derek broke out in a smile. "We're not trapped after all. All we have to do is break through that wall and find out what's on the other side."

"That should be easy enough," said Joe, cocking his fist. His arm shot forward and he punched a hole directly through the papier-mâché wall. Even as his fist cut through the flimsy material, the wall seemed to disintegrate. It fell into hundreds of shapeless pieces, which rained down on top of Joe like confetti.

At the same instant, the floor that he and the

others were standing on seemed to tilt forward sharply.

The five teenagers yelled as they found themselves thrown forward—tumbling down a steep ramp, head over heels.

11 Let There Be Light!

The downhill trip seemed to last forever.

The floor of the old mine was slick and steep. The lantern flew out of Derek's hand and disappeared somewhere down the slope. The group tumbled over and over in the darkness.

Finally, they reached the bottom of the slope. Dazed and bruised, the five teenagers lay on the floor for several minutes in silence.

"Anybody see the lantern?" asked Joe finally.

"I think so," said Derek. "There's a dim glow over in that direction."

"I can't see where you're pointing," said Joe. "It's too dark."

"Doesn't matter." Derek grunted as he struggled to his feet. "I'll get the lantern."

"What happened?" asked Pete. "The floor seemed to fall out from under us."

"I think the Secret Wizard Master rigged some kind of trick platform underneath us," said Frank. "When Joe punched a hole through the wall, it triggered some mechanism that tilted the platform and sent us rolling down the slope."

"Sounds like a pretty expensive setup," said Win. "Who's financing this Secret Wizard Master, anyway?"

"It doesn't have to be all *that* expensive," said Joe. "Maybe the Secret Wizard Master has henchmen."

"Henchmen?" asked Pete.

"That's true," said Frank. "We don't know that he's working alone. Instead of a mechanism under the platform, maybe there were one or two guys waiting for a signal. When it came, they could have pulled a couple of wedges out from under the platform. If the platform was mounted on wheels, the whole thing would have collapsed once the wedges were removed."

"If there are henchmen," asked Win, "where are they?"

"Who knows?" said Joe. "This place is dark and there are a lot of passages."

"I've got the lantern," said Derek as he rejoined the group. "At least we won't have to feel our way around in the dark."

"Glory be!" shouted Joe as the light from the lantern filled the room. "I can see again! It's a miracle!"

"Maybe not," said Frank. "I wonder how much

100

longer the batteries in that lantern can hold out. We might find ourselves in permanent darkness if we don't find a way out soon."

"Or find some new batteries," added Joe.

"Yuck," said Pete. "There are stains all over my clothes. Somebody must have greased that slide we just came down."

"Yeah, I'm covered with it, too," said Joe.

"Everybody up," said Derek. "Let's keep looking for that exit."

Pete stood and walked to a small pedestal in the middle of the room. Mounted on the pedestal was a large chest. "Well, here's another one," he said wearily.

"Let's take a look," said Win, walking to the chest. "There might be more batteries inside." He pulled on the lid, then fiddled for a moment with the latch. "I think it's locked," he said finally.

"What do you mean, locked?" asked Joe. "With a key?"

"No," said Win, examining the latch. "It's a combination lock."

"What are we going to do?" asked Pete. "We don't know the combination."

"Be patient," said Win. "There's a scroll attached to the chest."

"With a combination written on it?" asked Frank.

"Not exactly," said Win. "But I think it's a clue to the combination. Listen.

" 'MY FIRST IS A DOZEN TO A MAN WITH
        DOUGH.

101

MY SECOND IS THE DISTANCE FOR
  PHEIDIPPIDES TO GO.
MY THIRD IS THE TIME THAT A REVOLU-
  TION TAKES.
MY FOURTH IS A JURY, FOR GOODNESS'
  SAKES!
MY FIFTH ARE STELLAR SISTERS, WITH
  HEAVENLY ALLURES.
PUT THEM ALL TOGETHER AND THE
  TREASURE IS YOURS.' "

"It sounds like a riddle," said Pete.

"That's exactly what it is," said Frank. "Each line of the poem must be a clue to one of the numbers of the combination."

"Meaning," said Joe, "that there must be five numbers in the combination."

"Right. Let's take them one at a time," said Frank. "What was the first line again?"

" 'My first is a dozen to a man with dough,' " repeated Win dutifully.

"A dozen is twelve," said Joe. "But why would it be different to a rich man?"

"A 'man with dough' doesn't necessarily mean a rich man," suggested Derek. "It could refer to somebody who cooks dough."

"A baker?" asked Pete.

"A baker's dozen!" shouted Frank. "A baker's dozen is thirteen, because a baker supposedly slips an extra donut into a dozen as a gift to the customer!"

"I've never had a baker do that for me," complained Joe.

"Never mind that," said Frank. "Try dialing a thirteen on the combination lock, Win. It must be the first number of the combination."

Win turned the dial of the lock. "I think I heard a click," he told the others. "That must have been the right number."

"Great!" said Frank. "Now what was the second line?"

" 'My second is the distance for Pheidippides to go,' " read Win.

"What in the world is a Pheidippides?" asked Joe.

"I don't know," said Frank. "It sounds Greek."

"It *is* Greek," said Derek. "Pheidippides was the runner who ran from Marathon to Athens to tell the Greeks that they'd won a famous battle. He dropped dead afterward."

"So how far did he run?" asked Joe.

"No one is quite sure," said Derek. "The whole story may be a legend. It may never have happened."

"There must be some kind of number that goes with it," said Frank.

"Well," said Derek, "the marathon races at the Olympics were inspired by Pheidippides."

"And a marathon is twenty-six miles long!" cried Joe.

"Twenty-six miles, three hundred eighty-five yards, to be exact," said Derek.

"Let's not be quite that exact," said Frank. "Win, try dialing a twenty-six."

103

"You got it," said Win, turning the dial. "I think I heard another click!"

"We're cooking now!" said Joe. "What's the next line?"

" 'My third is the time that a revolution takes,' " said Win.

"That should be easy," said Joe. "How long did the American Revolution take?"

"Well," said Pete, "it started in 1775."

"Yeah, but when did it end?" asked Frank.

"Um, maybe I should have paid closer attention in history class," said Joe. "I think I was memorizing football plays the day we covered that."

"General Cornwallis surrendered in 1781," said Derek, "but the Treaty of Paris wasn't signed until 1783."

"Why didn't I just ask you in the first place?" said Joe. "Is there anything you *don't* know?"

"That makes it either five years or seven years," said Frank. "Which is it?"

"We don't even know if the Secret Wizard Master is talking about the American Revolution. Maybe he's referring to the French Revolution or the Mexican Revolution or some other revolution," said Derek.

"Wow," said Joe. "Maybe this one isn't so easy."

"What if he's referring to a different *kind* of revolution?" suggested Pete.

Derek snapped his fingers. "Of course! He must be talking about the revolution of the earth around its axis!"

"Which takes twenty-four hours!" cried Frank. "Win, try twenty-four for the next number!"

Win did so. "Another click!" he said.

"Two more to go," Derek said. "What's next, Win?"

" 'My fourth is a jury, for goodness' sakes!' "

"Let's see," said Frank. "How many people on a jury?"

" 'Twelve good men and true,' " answered Derek.

"What about women?" asked Joe.

"It's just an expression," said Derek. "It refers to both men and women."

"What does 'for goodness' sakes' have to do with it?" asked Pete.

"It rhymes," said Frank. "How about twelve for the next number, Win?"

"We've got another click," Win said.

"We're on a roll," said Joe. "What's the last clue, Win?"

" 'My fifth are stellar sisters, with heavenly allures,' " Win read.

"Hmmm," said Joe. "*Stellar* means 'star.' Could he be talking about movie stars?"

"What movie stars are sisters?" asked Pete.

"How would I know?" asked Joe. "I only watch the movies, I don't read the credits. Or the fan magazines."

"You're on the wrong track," said Derek. "I think he's talking about real stars, the kind you see in the sky. There's a group of stars called the Pleiades, which in Greek myth were the seven daughters of

Atlas. The stars are sometimes called the Seven Sisters."

"Seven!" said Frank. "That's your next number, Win."

Win turned the dial. "And now the lock should open . . . Yes! Got it!"

He pulled the lock off the chest. "Here goes," he said. "I'm going to open it."

"After all that work," said Joe, "there had better be something pretty special in that chest!"

Win grabbed the top of the chest with both hands and pulled up. Suddenly, as the lid came open, the sides of the chest fell away. Inside was a large spotlight, which abruptly turned on. A blinding light filled the room.

"Ow!" shouted Joe. "I can't see!"

"I can't, either," said Derek. "That light's painful!"

"Everybody close your eyes and turn the other way!" shouted Frank. "If you stare at that light too long, you'll lose your night vision."

"I've already lost it!" said Joe. "Even when I look the other way, everything is black."

"We've got to turn it off somehow!" said Pete.

"Move backward toward it," suggested Frank. "Maybe we can kick a hole in the glass."

"I'll do it," said Joe. "Everybody else stand still."

Suddenly a bloodcurdling scream echoed through the room. A second later it was choked off into silence.

"Who was that?" cried Frank. "What happened?"

"It wasn't me," said Joe.

"Or me," said Derek.

"I'm okay," said Pete.

"Where's Win?" asked Frank.

"Win, are you here?" cried Pete.

There was the sound of breaking glass as Joe kicked through the glass cover of the light, then darkness returned.

"I'm still blind," said Pete.

"Give it a minute," said Derek. "It'll take a while for the afterimages to fade away."

"I was looking in the other direction when the light came on," said Frank. "I think I'm getting my vision back already."

"What do you see?" asked Joe. "Is Win here?"

"No," said Frank. "I don't see him anywhere. But I do see something else."

"What?" asked Pete.

"There's something on the floor next to the chest where Win was standing."

"So what is it?" asked Joe.

"I'm not sure," said Frank. "But it looks like a pool of blood."

12 The Treasure of
the Dwarven King

After about five minutes the others in the group had regained their vision. Frank and Joe carefully examined the dark pool next to the chest and concluded that it was probably blood, though they couldn't be absolutely sure.

"So the Secret Wizard Master has claimed another victim!" said Joe.

"Poor Win!" said Frank. "He was standing right in the middle of us, but we couldn't help him."

"I think we should go back!" said Pete, his voice shaking and frightened. "If we go deeper into this mine, the same thing could happen to the rest of us!"

"I'd like to remind you," said Derek, "that we *can't* go back. There's no way to get across the abyss. And since the Secret Wizard Master literally greased

the slide that brought us down here, there's no way we can even go back to the last room."

Pete looked crestfallen. "I guess you're right. We have to go deeper, no matter what the risk."

"Believe me," said Frank, "if I thought we could get back out the front entrance to this place, I'd help you climb that slide myself. But we really don't have any choice."

"So where do we go next?" asked Joe.

"I guess we go forward," said Derek. "But beyond this point, things may well get worse."

"Talking about it won't make it any better," said Frank. "Let's plunge on before the light runs out."

"I think the bulb's getting dimmer already," said Derek. "We'd better hurry."

With grim determination, the group followed Derek deeper into the tunnel. The ceiling sloped down gradually above their heads and the walls seemed to grow closer together as they walked. The lantern light grew visibly dimmer.

"Pretty soon we'll have to crawl," said Joe. "This ceiling's already scraping my head."

"Pretty soon we'll be feeling our way in the dark," said Frank, "whether we're crawling or not. I don't like this one little bit."

"I . . . I'm getting scared," said Pete.

"Well, as long as everybody else is admitting to their fears, I have to say that I'm getting a little frightened myself," said Joe. "What about you, Derek?"

"Scared?" said Derek. "Me?"

"Derek!" said Joe forcefully.

"Oh, all right," Derek said with a laugh. "I'm scared. Who wouldn't be? In fact, I've been scared all along."

"I'll second that," said Joe. "But I guess being scared won't get us out of here. Even if the lantern goes out, we'll keep looking for the exit. And if we don't find it, somebody will eventually come and get us out."

"If the Secret Wizard Master doesn't get us first," Frank said.

"You're just trying to cheer us up," said Joe.

"And doing a pretty poor job of it," said Derek.

"What's this?" said Frank, staring ahead past Derek. "It looks like the tunnel goes straight up."

"Not quite," said Derek, "but it gets pretty steep here. Let's hope the passage is climbable."

"Let's climb and find out," said Joe. "We'll have to get down on all fours, anyway. The ceiling's too close to our heads."

The four teenagers began to crawl slowly up the steeply rising passage. When they reached the top, they discovered that the passage immediately started back down again.

"This would make a terrific roller coaster," Pete said.

"I wish it rolled and coasted," said Joe. "I'm going to have calluses on my hands and knees."

"If that's all we come out of here with," said Frank, "we can count ourselves lucky."

"At least it's downhill here," said Derek. "Ready to slide again?"

"Ready!"

"Who-o-o-o-o-ah!" shouted Joe, as they slid down the bumpy incline. Their feet touched bottom seconds later. The light from the lantern was so dim that they could barely discern the passage in front of them.

"I think the passage ends here," said Derek, peering into the darkness. "I hope this isn't a dead end."

"Look!" said Pete, pointing at a shadowy area on the floor. "I think that's a mine shaft."

"It is," said Joe, crawling to the edge of the hole and peering inside. The shaft was filled with murky shadows, but there was something running along one side. "I think there's a ladder leading down."

"You're right," said Frank, stooping beside the shaft and reaching into it. "It feels sturdy, too. I guess we'll have to climb down it."

"Hurry up," said Derek. "The lantern's almost out."

"I'm hurrying," said Frank, grabbing the ladder and climbing down the shaft. The others followed as quickly as they could.

At the bottom of the shaft was a large room, at least as large as the room where they had originally entered the mine. It was impossible to tell precisely how large the room was because the lantern was nearly out and most of the room was lost in shadows.

Suddenly the room filled with light, drowning out the feeble illumination of the bulb in the lantern. Heavy light fixtures hung from the ceiling far above, shining brightly on the floor below. In the light it was obvious that the room was larger than they had at

111

first thought, larger than any of the rooms they had been in so far.

"What in the world—?" shouted Joe.

"Where are we?" said Frank. "What is this place? Look at all that stuff!"

Frank gestured around the room. Piled on the floor and occupying more than half the room were hundreds of large brown boxes and crates. Mixed in with the boxes were dozens of incongruous pieces of expensive-looking merchandise: televisions, stereos, VCRs, microwave ovens, even home computer systems. Everything glistened with a look of pristine newness.

Joe's mouth fell open. "The Treasure of the Dwarven King," he said quietly.

"You've been hanging around Win too long," suggested Derek.

"No," said Frank. "He's right. This must be the treasure the Secret Wizard Master referred to. Win said that the goal of the new scenario was to find the Treasure of the Dwarven King at the bottom of a cavern. And this must be it!"

"I'd hoped that the treasure would be an exit," said Derek. "Do you suppose there might be one of those around here, too?"

"That's possible," said an unfamiliar voice from one side of the room.

Frank and the others looked up to see a dark-clad figure with short-cropped red hair standing atop a rock, looking down at them. Next to him, on the floor, stood a figure with brown hair, dressed entirely in black. Both were tall, heavyset, and in their

middle to late twenties. The redhead had a cocky smile on his face, while the other glared balefully at the group. Both held guns aimed at the group below.

"Welcome to the party," said the first figure. "We've been waiting for hours. We thought you'd never get here."

"But now that you're here," said the second figure, "you won't be leaving—alive."

13 The Secret Wizard Master

"Who are you?" asked Frank.

"Are you guys the Secret Wizard Masters?" said Joe.

The two men looked at each other. "I don't know what a secret Wizard Master is," said the man in black, "but I suppose it might be us. Come on. We've got something to show you." He reached into his pocket, pulled out a gun, and gestured toward the pile of boxes.

"You want us to walk over to those boxes?" Joe asked.

"Walk behind them," said the redhead. "Don't try to get away, not that you'd know where to go if you did. We'll be right behind you."

The four teenagers did as they were told. There

114

was a narrow space behind the boxes, submerged in shadow. Inside the space was a metal cage. Sitting in the cage were three people. Behind the cage was a large color television, showing an old movie. The people in the cage, who had been watching the movie, swiveled around as the group approached. Joe Hardy immediately recognized a stocky figure on the other side of the bars.

"Chet!" shouted Joe. "You're okay!"

"I'm locked in a cage, starving to death, watching a videotape of a lousy movie I've seen five times before," growled Chet. "If you call that okay, I guess I am, yeah."

"What happened to you?" asked Frank. "How did you get here?"

"The two stooges here," said Chet, nodding toward the pair of strangers, "dragged me down a mine shaft by my feet. They even brought their own ladder. Next thing I knew, they were tossing me in this cage."

"That's Barry Greenwald," said Pete, looking at the second figure in the cage. "You're the one we came to this place looking for, Barry."

"I know," the boy said quietly. "Tim told me all about it."

"Hey, that's Tim Partridge!" exclaimed Derek, studying the third occupant of the cage. "What are you doing here, Tim? We thought you'd gone home."

"I never made it," said Tim in a shaky voice. "It's a long story."

"We have plenty of time," said a new voice. "If you'd like to hear the story, I'd be happy to tell it."

The teenagers turned at the sound of the voice. A third figure stood between the two gunmen.

It was Win Thurber.

"Win!" shouted Pete. "You're okay, too! But . . . but why aren't you in the cage with the others?"

Win laughed. "I'm claustrophobic. I hate closed-in places."

"I don't understand," said Pete.

"I think I do," said Frank.

"Right," said Joe. "You're the Secret Wizard Master, aren't you, Win?"

"Bingo!" said Win with a smile. "Now I see why you guys are considered such great detectives! Give you a couple of subtle clues, like a gun stuck in your face, and you've got all the answers!"

"We're smart that way," said Frank.

"So why did you trap us in this mine, Win?" asked Derek. "I've always thought of you as a little flaky, but not downright twisted."

"Why don't we let our great detectives figure it out?" said Win. "The evidence is staring them right in the face." He gestured toward the stacks of boxes piled on the floor.

"Stolen merchandise?" asked Frank.

"You're getting warm," said Win.

"From Bergmeyer's Department Store?" asked Joe.

"Give the man a Kewpie doll!" said Win, laughing.

"You and your friends here—your henchmen—have been robbing the department store blind and storing the merchandise in the bottom of this old mine," said Frank.

116

"That's right," said Win. "You see, there *is* more to my life than games."

"What do you do with the merchandise after you steal it?" asked Joe. "The three of you couldn't possibly use that many microwave ovens."

"We leave it here until it cools off—that is, until nobody's looking for it anymore. Then we sell it on the black market. That's how I make my living. It takes a lot of money to keep me in games—computer games, board games, all that stuff."

"I thought you were a student at Bayport High," Frank said.

"I dropped out years ago," said Win. "I would have graduated by now, anyway. But I look young for my age and telling people that I'm a high-school student saves me from embarrassing explanations about what I do for a living. Besides, who needs an education? I've got all the money I need."

"Is this the kind of life you want to live?" asked Frank. "The life of a common thief?"

"There's nothing common about me," said Win. "Though I guess it's fair to call me a thief."

"Don't flatter yourself, Win," said Derek with a sneer.

"How do *we* figure into this?" asked Joe.

"Right," said Derek. "Was it really necessary to trap us in this mine and try to kill us?"

"No," said Win. "We could have killed you right off the bat. But it *was* necessary that we do something about you, before things got out of hand."

"Don't tell me," said Frank. "Barry Greenwald

saw something down here that he wasn't supposed to see."

"That's right," said Win. "Barry got a little too nosy around the dungeon. Want to tell them about it, Barry?"

A short, black-haired boy stared out between the bars of the cage with mournful eyes. "I . . . I was exploring the dungeon one day last month. I'd never been down on the lower levels and I just thought I'd take a quick look, then get out. I took an old lantern with me and crawled down this tunnel . . . and I found myself in this big room. There were all these boxes and all this stuff piled up and these two guys walking around. They were talking about stolen goods and selling the stuff to a fence or something. I saw they had guns. I got out before they could see me. I thought about calling the police, but I was afraid the police would close up the dungeon if I told them about it. That's why I didn't tell anybody. But it worried me. And that's when I made a big mistake."

"What was the mistake, Barry?" asked Pete softly.

"I told Win about it. I didn't know he had anything to do with the guys I saw down here. Win told me not to mention what I'd seen to anyone. He said he'd check it out quietly. But he never did anything. So I told him I was going to talk it over with Tim. I was going to tell Tim about it this afternoon. I even went to the park to wait for him. Then Win showed up and he had these two guys with him. They grabbed me, brought me to the dungeon, and locked me up in this cage."

"What about you, Tim?" asked Derek. "How'd

118

you wind up down here? The last time I saw you, you were headed home to your parents."

"I . . . I started home on my bicycle," Tim said. "And these two guys in a car tried to run me off the road. I fell off my bike, and they got out of the car and forced me to get inside with them. They had guns."

"Was it these two guys here?" Derek asked, pointing toward the gunmen.

"Yeah," said Tim. "They're the ones."

"How long have you had this racket going, Win?" asked Joe.

"A couple of years," said Win. "Since shortly after I started the job at Bergmeyer's. My father lost his job and then my parents got divorced. My mother had almost no income, and I had to make a living somehow. One day I was working in the store and I caught these two shoplifting." He gestured toward the two men standing next to him. "Steve and Mike," he said, indicating the redhead and the brunette respectively. "I was going to call security and turn them in, but they made a deal with me. If I'd help them steal merchandise, they'd give me a cut of the profits."

"Couldn't pass it up, huh, Win?" said Derek.

"No," said Win. "I needed the money, Derek. I needed it badly. I'll bet you've never been in that situation."

"No, but even if I was, I wouldn't steal."

"That's your choice," said Win. "But I made a different choice. And it worked out well. Eventually I got a transfer to Bergmeyer's warehouse. Now we

119

can swipe whole truckloads of merchandise. I'll never need money again. Pretty soon I hope to set my mother up in a new house and get my own place, too."

"I think the store might notice all that merchandise missing," said Joe.

"They probably will," said Win. "But Bergmeyer's is part of a national chain and they have a huge inventory. If we play our cards right, they'll never be able to pin down which stores the thefts are centered around. I expect to be promoted to a low-level management job soon, and then I'll have access to the national warehouses."

"Won't people wonder where all your money came from?" asked Frank.

"They might," said Win. "So I'm going to make it look like a rich uncle left it to us. I've paid off a crooked lawyer. He's drawing up the papers now. It'll all seem perfectly fair and square."

"How did you happen to set up this little underground warehouse?" asked Joe.

"Steve, Mike, and I would drive our stolen trucks out here into the woods and unload them," said Win. "We'd meet with a fence—that's the guy who pays us money for the stolen goods—in the woods and he'd cart the stuff away for us. One day he told us that we were glutting the market, that he had too much of our stuff on hand and it was too hot to sell. He wanted us to hold off for a while, let the merchandise cool down."

"So you went looking for a cave to put it in?" asked Pete.

"No," said Win. "We found this place by accident. We were standing around in the woods, trying to figure out what we were going to do with all this merchandise that the fence wouldn't take, and Mike stumbled on the entrance to the mine. We explored it for a while, until we found this room, and we knew right away that it was the perfect place to store the goods."

"How did a crook like you end up playing Wizards and Warriors?" asked Joe.

"Hey, all that stuff I told you about liking games is true," said Win. "Before my father lost his job, he bought me all the games I wanted, and I spent every free minute playing them. Then, after the divorce, we had to sell most of them. It really hurt."

"So you started playing Wizards and Warriors to compensate for all the games you'd lost?" asked Frank.

"Not exactly. We had set up our little, uh, warehouse down here in the mine, right? A couple of months later, we saw some guys snooping around in the upper rooms. We investigated and found out that they were game players who had come here to play Wizards and Warriors. They started decorating the mine with chests and doors and stuff. Steve and Mike wanted to chase them out of the place . . . or worse. But I thought that would be a little too suspicious. It might call attention to us. So I agreed to join the Wizards and Warriors club to keep an eye on the players, make sure that they didn't stumble on our little operation down here."

"A dirty job," said Derek sarcastically, "but somebody had to do it."

"It was the best thing I ever did," said Win, "except for teaming up with Steve and Mike. I *loved* the game. I couldn't stop playing. I learned everything about it that I could. Then Barry stumbled on this room and that was the end of it."

"You had to get rid of Barry?" said Frank.

"I had to get rid of all of you," said Win. "Everybody who knew about the dungeon. It's too bad that you and your brother had to be at the game session this afternoon, Frank. I wish you hadn't been caught up in all this."

"But why the Secret Wizard Master business?" asked Joe. "There must be easier ways to get rid of people."

"Yes," said Win with a smile, "but they're nowhere near as much fun. The Secret Wizard Master business, as you call it, was my idea. A way of getting in one last game of Wizards and Warriors before I disposed of the whole club. It was the best game of Wizards and Warriors I've ever played!"

"What are you going to do with us now?" asked Derek.

Win broke out in a grin. "I'm going to take you all for a swim."

"A swim?" asked Frank. "Underground?"

"Sure," said Win. "Follow me. Steve, Mike, you guys let the other kids out of the cage and bring them along."

"I have a feeling we're not going to like whatever it is he's going to show us," said Joe.

"You and me both," said Frank.

Win led the group back around the pile of boxes. He pointed toward the other end of the room, where the walls narrowed. There were no lights at that end of the room, at least none that were turned on; only shadows were visible. Win pulled a large electrical switch mounted on the wall. Light filled the far end of the room.

"Uh-oh," said Joe. "I think I see what he's talking about."

"Come on," said Win. "Take a closer look."

At the far end of the room the floor ended abruptly, in a sheer cliff. Below the cliff was water, an underground lake, which stretched for about a hundred yards before disappearing into a tunnel in the far wall.

"Your own private swimming pool," said Joe.

"I don't swim here," said Win. "Too cold."

"This must come from the reservoir," said Pete.

"If that water's from the reservoir," said Derek, "why isn't the water level higher? In fact, why isn't this entire room flooded?"

Win pointed to one of the walls that flanked the lake. The wall was covered with thick wooden boards, nailed together and supported by heavy wooden struts, some of which disappeared into the water of the underground lake, some of which were mounted on the cliff itself.

"The guys who built this mine did a better job than they realized," Win said. "Apparently they boarded up this room to protect it from the reservoir, building a makeshift dam to keep the water out.

They probably didn't expect it to hold for long—maybe just long enough for them to finish their mining operations and get their equipment out—but it's still holding up today. There's just enough leakage to keep the lake from going dry. The water level is as low as it is because the lake drains into an underground river, which runs underneath much of this mine."

"Where does that tunnel lead?" asked Frank, pointing across the water.

"That's the exit you've been looking for all night," said Win. "We use it to bring the merchandise in and out. Our boat's anchored down there."

Win pointed to a small wooden raft moored to the edge of the cliff. Two or three empty cardboard boxes were scattered about on its grimy deck.

"Exactly why are you showing us all of this?" asked Frank.

"I'm afraid I'm going to have to ask all of you—you should excuse the expression—to go jump into the lake," Win replied.

"Aren't you afraid we'll swim out through that tunnel?" asked Derek.

"Not at all," said Win. "Remember, we have guns. Anybody who swims near the exit will be shot. And don't try swimming underwater. You'd never make it far enough. And you'd be surprised how far a bullet travels through water."

"What's the point?" asked Joe. "Do you expect us to soak to death?"

"Like I said, the water is cold," Win told him. "You'll pass out from hypothermia within fifteen

124

minutes and sink like bricks. It'll be years before your bodies are found, if they ever are. We'll have moved our operations out of Bayport long before then. The authorities will assume you died in a tragic accident, playing around in an old mine. Accidents like that happen dozens of times each year."

"I'd just as soon cancel this swimming trip," said Joe.

"Me, too," said Frank.

"Ditto," said Chet.

"I'm not giving you that choice," said Win. "You'll notice that Steve and Mike have guns that are loaded with *bullets.* One way or another, you're going in that water. I hope you'll be cooperative and line up at the water's edge, so you can go in one at a time. Joe, how'd you like to be first?"

"I think I'll pass on that," said Joe.

"Sorry," said Win. "But it's your turn, Joe. Step over to the cliff or I'll have to ask Steve to take desperate action."

Joe stared distastefully at the redheaded gunman, then walked reluctantly to the water's edge. "You want me to jump?" he asked glumly.

"Jump or I push you," said Win.

"Sure you don't want to join me, Win?" Joe asked.

"Stop stalling," said Win. "Just jump."

The redheaded gunman waved his gun menacingly in Joe's direction and smiled broadly. Joe looked down at the dark waters below. He held his arms out in front of his body and prepared to jump into the frigid waters.

125

14 Flood!

"Hey, Win!" said Frank urgently.

"What now?" snapped Win. "It'll be your turn in a minute, Frank. Be patient."

"You're forgetting something, Win," Frank said insistently.

"Forgetting something?" said Win. "What are you talking about?"

"Well, that was a brilliant game of Wizards and Warriors you played with us in the dungeon this afternoon," Frank said. "I thought you'd want to tell us a few things about it, before you make us jump into the water."

Win laughed. "Is that all? Why would I want to tell you more than I already have?"

"I thought you'd want a chance to brag," said Frank. "Explain how you hoodwinked us, how you set the dungeon up the way you did. I'm sure your

friends Steve and Mike aren't especially interested in games like Wizards and Warriors. Not the way Derek and Pete are, anyway. Or Chet and Barry and Tim."

"You're just stalling for time," said Win, though it was obvious from his tone of voice that he was intrigued by what Frank had said.

"That's true," said Frank. "I'd like a few extra minutes to live, and I'm sure the others would, too. Why don't you give us those extra minutes, Win? In return, you can tell us about how you trounced us in Wizards and Warriors."

"Well," said Win. "I suppose a few more minutes won't hurt. . . ."

"You told us you'd get rid of them as soon as they found their way down here," said Mike. "Are you going back on your promise?"

"Lighten up, Mike," said Win. "It took me a long time to set this thing up and I'd like to talk about it a little, that's all."

"Just hurry it up," said Mike irritably.

"I will. Okay, Frank, you can have your extra few minutes. What do you want to know?"

"Anything you want to tell us," said Frank. "How did you think up that business about the colored keyholes and the colored keys? That was pretty ingenious."

"You think so?" said Win eagerly. "Yeah, I thought that was pretty clever, too. It's something I saw in a computer game once, where you had to find your way through this Egyptian tomb and there were these keys and locks in different colors . . ."

"Actually, I thought it was a pretty stupid idea,"

said Joe. "I've played that computer game and I recognized it right off. You couldn't even come up with an original idea, could you?"

Win glared fiercely at Joe. "You can stay out of this!" he said. "Maybe I'll make you jump into the water first, *then* I'll tell this story."

"Sorry," said Joe. "I'll keep my mouth shut."

"Forgive my brother," said Frank with a smile. "He gets in these moods every now and then. I thought the business with the keys was terrific, Win. Very imaginative."

"Why, thank you, Frank," said Win.

"And the pool of blood," Frank said. "Very realistic. It really had me fooled. Where'd you get that stuff, anyway?"

Win grinned broadly. "I picked it up in a costume shop. It goes with their Dracula costume. I thought it was pretty neat, too!"

"Oh, and the papier-mâché wall," Frank went on. "That must have taken a long time to build. In fact, this whole thing must have taken quite a while. Where did you find the time?"

"Well, I do tend to think ahead," said Win, with a modest smile. "That's what makes me such a good game player. As soon as Barry stumbled onto the warehouse, I knew I had to set up my real-life game of Wizards and Warriors. So I started building the stuff. The wall took about a week, with another week for the platform underneath. And you guys were right about the way the platform worked, by the way. Steve and Mike were stationed next to the platform,

so that they could pull out the wedges the moment you guys broke through the wall."

"I guess that must have been pretty amusing for you, Win," said Frank. "Standing in that room, with everybody thinking they were trapped forever between the abyss and the wall. You were the only one who knew that the wall was only papier-mâché, that we could get through anytime we wanted to."

Win laughed. "It *was* pretty funny, now that you mention it. When you begged the Secret Wizard Master to reveal his identity, so that we could escape from the trap, I almost broke out laughing. I knew that you'd eventually figure out that the wall was papier-mâché. Of course, I had to give you a couple of hints first."

"Glad to see that you respect our intelligence," said Joe. "I think this whole thing is sick, Win. In fact, I think you've got a twisted mind. I notice that you made yourself the 'victim' of some of your own traps. You like flirting with danger, don't you? Well, I think you're just an egotistical show-off. And I don't think you're wrapped too tight, either."

"Easy, Joe," cautioned Frank.

"I think I'll enjoy seeing you sink into the lake, Joe," said Win. "You've got a pretty nasty personality."

"Joe's all right," said Frank. "I guess he just got up on the wrong side of the bed this morning."

"I wouldn't have gotten up at all if I'd known I was going to meet Win here," said Joe. "He makes me ill!"

"I've had about enough of you, Hardy," said Win sharply. "You've had your few extra minutes. Now it's time to go into the lake."

"What's the matter, Win?" said Joe. "I've just insulted you. Aren't you man enough to defend your reputation? Or are you just going to let your gun-toting friends intimidate me into jumping into freezing water? That's the coward's way out."

"What do you mean, defend my reputation?" asked Win.

"The way Derek did earlier, when I insulted him," said Joe.

Derek's eyes lit up. "Right, Win. Why don't you challenge Joe to a duel? You've got a sword. I'll lend Joe mine."

Win glanced from Joe to Derek suspiciously. "You don't believe I can handle myself with a sword, do you? That shows what you know. Okay, I'll duel with Joe. But don't think that the rest of you can pull something funny while we fight. Steve and Mike'll be keeping an eye on you."

"That's fine with me," said Joe. "Derek, give me the sword."

"Coming right up," said Derek, tossing the sword to Joe. Joe caught it easily by the hilt.

"You think those sword fighting lessons that Derek gave you will help you, don't you, Joe?" said Win. "I think you've got a surprise coming. We'll fight right over here, next to the water. Loser's the first one to go into the lake." He laughed.

"Sounds okay to me," said Joe, moving to the small patch of empty ground Win had indicated. Win held

his sword out in front of his chest and prepared to fight.

Joe came at him with a quick lunge, but Win sidestepped it. Joe was surprised by the speed of Win's movement. Maybe Win did have some experience at sword fighting!

"Not all of the games I've played have been intellectual," said Win. "When I was a kid, my father bought me fencing lessons. I was pretty good at it."

"Now you tell me," muttered Joe.

Win thrust skillfully at Joe, who was barely able to raise his sword in time to deflect the blow. Win smiled smugly as Joe began to sweat.

"Don't get too cocky, Win," said Joe. "Overconfidence has lost more than one fight."

"I'll be careful," said Win. "Why don't you try to hit me with that sword again, Joe?"

"Gladly," said Joe, lunging at Win a second time. Win knocked Joe's sword aside with the edge of his sword.

"Don't let him scare you, Joe," said Derek.

"Don't worry," said Frank. "My brother knows how to handle himself."

I hope so! thought Joe desperately. Now that I've got myself into this situation, I've got to get myself back out alive!

Win came at Joe rapidly, stabbing at him with a series of short thrusts. Within seconds Joe found himself turned with his back to the lake—which was probably exactly where Win wanted him!

"I hope you're a better swimmer than you are a

sword fighter," said Win. "In a second, you'll be carrying Derek's sword to the bottom of the lake."

The Sicilian Switchback! thought Joe. It's my only hope! Win wasn't watching when Derek taught me that trick. Maybe I can catch him off guard with it.

Win moved in closer, preparing to deal the blow that would knock Joe into the lake. Joe looked at the water nervously out of the corner of his eye, automatically measuring the distance that separated him from the edge of the cliff. It was no more than two feet. He had to make his move now; there was no room left to maneuver.

Grinning, Win poked his sword at Joe again and again. Joe knocked it aside awkwardly with his own sword, afraid to move backward any farther. Then, remembering Derek's instructions, he manipulated his sword directly underneath Win's. As rapidly as possible, he brought it up and down in a quick W-shaped motion, forcing the point toward the hilt of Win's sword.

I've got it! Joe thought.

Then, more rapidly than Joe could follow, Win flashed his own sword up and down, bringing it up underneath Joe's sword and snatching it away by the hilt. Joe's sword flew into the air and vanished into the lake with a sharp splash.

"The Sicilian Switchback!" crowed Win, laughing sharply. "That trick's so old it has whiskers on it! I didn't know anybody used that one anymore!"

Joe glanced desperately at Derek, who had a crestfallen look on his face. Without the sword, Joe was seemingly defenseless against Win's assault.

"You really are a lousy sword fighter, Joe," said Win pityingly, raising his sword and preparing to push Joe into the lake.

"I may be lousy with a sword," said Joe, "but that doesn't mean I can't fight!"

Joe brought his booted foot up in a sharp kick, catching Win right below the knee. With a yell, Win leapt back, hopping wildly as he realized his left foot wouldn't take his weight.

"Good going!" shouted Derek.

"Way to go, Joe!" cheered Frank.

Tottering backward, Win went right into one of the struts supporting the wooden dam, falling heavily against it. With an earsplitting crack, the strut snapped into two pieces, and Win toppled off the cliff, falling into the lake below.

Pete started involuntarily. "Win!" he shouted.

"Look over there!" shouted Derek. "The dam!"

With the strut disabled, the end of the wooden dam closest to the cliff began to bulge away from the wall. Water came pouring over it, in a dark waterfall.

"The whole thing's going to give way!" shouted Steve, the redheaded gunman. "We're going to drown!"

15 Everybody into the Lake

"The raft!" shouted Mike. "We've got to get to the raft!"

"What about these kids?" asked Steve frantically. "What do we do with them?"

"Forget the kids!" Mike yelled. "Just get in the raft and get out of here!"

"Hey!" shouted Frank to the other teenagers. "We can't let these crooks get away!"

"Oh, yes, we can," said Derek. "I'm getting in the raft myself!"

"Oh, no, you're not," said Mike, rounding on the group, gun in hand. "You're staying here!"

"We'll drown," groaned Chet.

"Tough luck," muttered Steve, rushing to the edge

134

of the cliff. There was a wooden ladder nailed to the cliffside, leading to the moored raft. Steve grabbed the ladder and started climbing down.

"Stay away from that raft!" shouted Joe, still standing next to the cliff. He swung his sword at Steve's head, hitting him sharply with the flat side of it. Steve grunted with pain and fell off the ladder, splashing into the water next to the raft. The gun flew out of his hand and disappeared into the lake.

"That's enough out of you, kid!" said Mike, turning toward Joe and pointing his gun at him.

"Whoops!" said Joe. "See you around, fella!" He turned and executed a graceful swan dive over the edge of the cliff, hitting the water next to Steve. Mike fired the gun a second too late. The bullet whizzed out over the lake and missed Joe by several feet.

With a loud bang, the torrent of water from the bulging dam struck the piles of cardboard boxes, knocking them helter-skelter around the room. Televisions were shattered into wood and metal shards, their picture tubes exploding with the impact. The television that the prisoners had been watching a moment earlier made sizzling noises as the water swept over it.

"Everybody into the lake!" shouted Frank. "Here comes the flood!"

"Gangway!" shouted Chet, jumping feetfirst off the cliff, nose pinched tightly between thumb and forefinger. The others followed him, while Mike scuttled down the ladder to the raft.

Joe, who had jumped into the water seconds

earlier, bobbed back to the surface in time to see a soaking wet Steve clawing his way out of the water and onto the raft.

"No way, pal!" Joe yelled, grabbing Steve by the neck and attempting to pull him back into the lake.

"Let go of him, kid!" bellowed Mike, leaping onto the raft. He swung his gun to cover Joe.

"Uh-oh," said Joe, letting go of Steve and diving back under the water.

Steve flopped onto the deck of the raft like a half-dead fish. Mike hastily untied the knot that kept the raft moored to the cliff. Then he grabbed a large wooden pole and pushed the raft toward the middle of the lake, just as a cascade of water came pouring over the cliffside.

"Brrrrrrr!" said Chet, bobbing to the surface of the lake. "This water's freezing!"

"I can't swim!" shouted a desperate, high-pitched voice. Barry Greenwald floundered frantically in the water as his friend Tim Partridge watched helplessly.

"Hang on, Barry," said Pete, swimming to the boy's side and grabbing him under the arms. "I've got you. Just be still and don't panic."

"We've got to get those guys off the raft," said Derek, his blond hair hanging down on his forehead in sopping wet strands. "I don't know how long we can stay afloat."

"Lots of luck," said Joe, reappearing next to the others. "That guy Mike still has his gun . . . and he looks as if he's willing to use it."

"Maybe we can swim to the tunnel," suggested Chet.

"With Mike taking potshots at us?" said Joe. "Not a chance."

"Yeah," said Frank. "These guys don't want us getting out of here alive. We know too much."

On the raft, Mike was helping Win pull himself out of the water. Win looked cold and bedraggled, the cocky self-confidence he had shown earlier almost completely gone. He collapsed on the deck of the raft to catch his breath.

"Maybe if we all attack the raft at once . . ." suggested Joe in a low voice. "Or maybe not."

"Do you suppose we can swim underneath the raft and tip it over?" whispered Chet.

"No," said Derek.

"Come on," said Joe. "There's got to be a way!"

"What are you kids talking about?" shouted Mike suspiciously. "If I see you heading in this direction, I'm going to nail you so full of bullet holes you'll look like sponges!"

"Nice guy," said Frank.

"I think my legs are starting to go numb," said Pete. "I don't know how much longer I can tread water."

"Okay," Joe said under his breath. "We've got to go after the raft."

"How?" asked Chet. "That caveman with the gun has his eyes on us like a hawk."

"We'll have to distract him," whispered Frank. "You talk to him, Chet. Joe and I will swim under the

137

raft and come up on the other side while he's not looking."

"He might notice that you're missing," said Chet.

"There are seven of us in the water, splashing like crazy. There's no way he can keep count, not if you do some fast talking and keep his mind on something else."

"Let's go, then," said Joe. "Before we all freeze to death."

"Remember, Chet," said Frank. "Just keep talking, about anything. And I know you can do *that.*"

Chet raised an eyebrow. "Thanks a heap. I'll do my best."

"Come on," said Joe. "Take a deep breath . . . and let's go!"

Joe and Frank each gulped a lungful of air, then slid beneath the surface. Chet watched them swim away underwater, then he turned toward the raft.

"Hey, Mike," he yelled. "We want to make a deal with you!"

"No deals," said Mike. "You don't have anything we want!"

"Are you sure?" said Chet. "You know that the police will be waiting for you when you get out of here, don't you?"

"What are you talking about?" asked Mike. "The police don't even know we're here."

"No," said Chet. "But they'll know right away when you walk out of here. Tim Partridge told his parents about the dungeon before he left for the meeting this afternoon and they probably have the

police scouring the area by now. Chances are, you'll run smack into them when you leave here."

"What?" said Tim. "I didn't—"

"—didn't know that all of this was going to happen when you talked to your parents!" said Chet, desperately finishing Tim's sentence. "But it's sure a good thing that you told them about this place, isn't it?"

Mike turned to Win, who was still lying on the deck of the raft. "Did you know about this?" he asked.

"They're bluffing," said Win. "Don't listen to them."

"How do we know you're telling the truth?" said Mike, turning back to Chet. "How do we know you're not just making this up to save your skins?"

"I guess you don't," said Chet. "But you don't have much of a choice. You can't be sure that what I'm telling you isn't true."

Behind the raft, Chet saw Frank and Joe slide out of the water, gasping silently for air. Mike, Steve, and Win were all staring directly at Chet and failed to notice the Hardys approaching on the other side of the raft.

"Suppose I do believe you," said Mike. "What are we supposed to do about it?"

"Give us the raft," said Chet. "We'll go out and tell the police that everything's okay, then we'll bring the raft back when the coast is clear."

"Hah!" laughed Mike. "We could never trust you to do that! If the police are really waiting for us, the

139

only way we'll get out of here is if we have hostages!"
He raised the gun and pointed it at Chet. "And the
only hostages in the vicinity are you kids!" He began
poling the raft toward the group of teenagers, holding the pole in one hand and his gun in the other.

Frank pulled himself out of the water and onto the
raft, followed seconds later by Joe. Steve and Win,
still lying bedraggled on the deck, looked up at them
in surprise.

"Look out, Mike!" shouted Win. "They're behind
you!"

Mike spun around, just in time to see Frank's fist
flying at him. The gun fell to the deck, where Steve
snatched it up. Joe gave Steve a swift kick in the
shoulder, knocking him into the water.

"Yay, Joe!" shouted Chet. "Yay, Frank! Give those
guys what they deserve!"

Win grabbed Joe around the legs and brought him
tumbling to the deck. Frank and Mike, their arms
locked together in a tight wrestling hold, fell off the
raft and into the water.

"Come on!" cried Chet, swimming toward the
raft. "Let's help them out!"

"This is what I call a fair fight," said Joe as he
grabbed Win by the scruff of the neck. "No swords!"
He cocked his arm back and punched Win squarely
on the jaw. Win fell back to the deck, stunned.

Frank and Mike splashed wildly in the water next
to the raft, each trying to dunk the other's head
beneath the water. Chet swam up behind Mike,
snapped his arm around Mike's neck, and pulled him
away from Frank.

"Okay, okay," cried Mike. "I surrender. You guys have got us!"

"You bet we've got you," said Frank, pulling himself back onto the raft. "Come on, Chet. Leave him in the water for now. When he's good and worn out, we'll give him and Steve a lift on the raft— before they freeze to death. Then we'll get the heck out of this place."

"I'm on my way," said Chet, swimming back to the raft. Mike tried to swim after him, but Frank poked him in the head with the wooden pole. One by one, the teenagers pulled themselves on board. Steve and Mike treaded water alongside. Win lay on the deck, still stunned.

"Where are we headed?" Joe asked.

"To the exit," said Frank. "The tunnel that Win showed us."

"What tunnel?" said Chet, staring at the far end of the lake. Where earlier the mouth of a tunnel had been visible in the cave wall, there was now only sheer rock, with water lapping against it.

Frank followed Chet's gaze. "The tunnel's gone!" he cried. "What happened to it?"

"The water's rising!" said Derek. "The exit's underwater now! We're trapped!"

16 Underwater Escape

"We'll have to swim underwater," said Frank. "If we're lucky, the tunnel will turn upward on the other side of the entrance, so that we can come up for air."

"And if we're not lucky?" asked Joe.

"Try not to think about it," said Frank.

"Or just concentrate on growing gills," suggested Derek.

"Barry," said Frank. "Do you think you can swim underwater long enough to get through the tunnel?"

"I can't swim at all," said Barry, a frightened look in his eyes.

"I'll help him," said Pete. "I'm a pretty good swimmer."

"Okay," said Frank. "Everybody else know how to swim?"

"I was county swimming champion last year," said Derek.

"I probably should have guessed that," said Frank. "Anybody else have a problem?"

Win stirred groggily on the deck. "What's happening? Where are we?"

"We're about to go for a swim," said Joe. "I hope you're good at holding your breath."

"What?" said Win. "Why don't you just push the raft out through the tunnel?"

"It's underwater, that's why," said Joe.

Win turned pale. "What are you going to do?" he asked.

"Swim for it," said Joe. "You're on your own now, Win."

"Ready?" said Frank to the others. "Let's go." He stood and dived into the water, the others following immediately after.

Frank swam to the far side of the lake. When he reached the cave wall, he reached out to touch it with his hands, as though to make sure that it was really solid. The others swam up beside him.

"The exit must be directly under here," Frank said. "Take a deep breath and swim straight down. If it doesn't look like the tunnel comes out anyplace, turn around and swim back in here before you run out of air."

"I'm scared," said Tim Partridge.

"So are we all," said Derek. "But we've got to get out of here somehow, before this whole room fills up with water. Let's start swimming before the water gets any deeper."

"Follow me," said Frank, filling his lungs with air. He bobbed above the surface for a moment, then dived under the water.

Swimming downward, he groped against the wall, trying to find an opening. Several feet above him, Joe did the same.

Suddenly Frank's hands detected an opening. The tunnel was about five feet below the surface, and more than wide enough to swim through. Frank could barely tell where he was as he entered the tunnel. Once inside, he was completely wrapped in darkness. He started to turn and look for Joe, then thought better of it.

Better not get turned around, he thought. He raised his hand above his head until he could feel the roof of the tunnel, then propelled himself forward with powerful breaststrokes.

Not far behind Frank, Joe also swam in pitch-darkness. He thought that he could feel the backwash of his brother's powerful swimming strokes from in front of him, then decided that that probably wasn't possible.

What if I get lost? he thought. He felt a sudden hint of panic deep in the pit of his stomach, but he fought it off. Panic and you'll *really* be lost, he thought.

The tunnel seemed to go on forever. In the lead,

Frank held his hand above his head every few seconds to see if the roof of the tunnel had moved upward, but it was still directly above him. His lungs ached with the desire for air.

Suddenly his hands touched something wooden. A ladder! He grabbed it and pulled himself upward. His head broke through the surface of the water and into the air.

He was in a mine shaft. A slight hint of moonlight poured down from somewhere above him. He climbed quickly upward.

Below him there was a splashing noise as someone else climbed out of the water. "Hey, Frank! Is that you?" shouted Joe's voice.

"Yeah!" Frank replied. "Glad to see you made it!"

"The others are right behind me," Joe said. "Where's this shaft lead to, anyway?"

"I don't know," said Frank. "I haven't reached the top yet."

Frank continued climbing. He could hear other voices beneath him now, as the rest of the group climbed out of the water. At the top of the ladder he emerged into fresh air. Climbing out of the shaft, he realized that he was on a hillside next to the Bayport Reservoir. About a hundred yards to his right, there was a chain-link fence, beyond which was a deserted road.

Joe climbed out of the shaft behind Frank. "Free at last!" he shouted. "Boy, it's good to smell fresh air again!"

"And see the sky!" cried Frank.

145

"And taste food!" added Chet, coming out of the shaft behind Joe. "You guys don't see anything to eat out here, do you?"

"No such luck, Chet," said Joe. "Too bad you're not thirsty. We've got lots of water. Boy, do we have lots of water!"

The others straggled out of the shaft after Chet, soaking wet but deliriously happy. "I don't care if they *do* close down the dungeon forever," said Pete, as he staggered out. "I never want to see the inside of that place again."

"Agreed," said Derek. "If they want to dynamite the entrance, I'll light the fuse."

"Hold it, you kids!" snapped a familiar voice. "Freeze right there!"

The group turned to see Steve, the redheaded gunman, standing at the mouth of the shaft, pointing a gun at them. "Nobody move!" shouted Steve. "You're all hostages, do you hear? We're not letting you go until we're safely out of Bayport!"

"Stick it in your ear, Steve," said Frank, walking toward the gunman. "You're not in charge anymore."

"Watch out, Frank!" said Joe. "He's got a gun!"

"I don't think there's much to worry about," said Frank, heedless of Steve's weapon.

"You asked for it!" said Steve. He pointed the gun at Frank and pulled the trigger. The gun made a soggy snapping sound.

"I don't think your gun's waterproof," said Frank, grabbing it away from the redheaded man and

146

tossing it down the hill. "On the other hand, I think *you're* all washed up."

Joe grabbed the rope that Win was wearing around his tunic and used it to secure Win's hands behind his back. Frank tied Steve's hands with Pete's sash. Derek produced a rope from his own costume and did the same with Mike.

"Hey!" shouted Chet, pointing toward the road. "There's a car coming!"

"It looks like a police cruiser!" shouted Joe. "Hey, officer! Up here! We need help!"

The cruiser pulled to the side of the road and a pair of police officers stepped out, guns at the ready. Frank and Joe raced to the fence to meet them.

"Um, officers," Frank said hesitantly, aware not only that he was drenched from head to toe but that several of the people behind him were wearing tunics and imitation chain mail. "You're not going to believe this, but we've been trapped all night in a medieval dungeon."

The two officers turned and looked at one another, then turned back to Frank and Joe.

"It's a long story," said Joe. "Believe me, it's a long story."

Two hours later, Frank and Joe walked out of the Bayport police station, heading for their van. Win Thurber had been released into his mother's custody, and Mike and Steve were stuck in a jail cell. Joe, Frank, and the other teenagers had been loaned dry clothing by generous police officers.

"It's after midnight!" Joe said. "Aunt Gertrude must be frantic!"

"Relax," said Frank. "I gave her a call as soon as we got here. And, yes, she's frantic. She called the police five times this evening to report us missing. Good thing she did, too, or that police cruiser might not have been patrolling the woods by the reservoir."

"I guess it'll be a while before we hear the end of this," said Joe.

"Probably," said Frank. "But, Aunt Gertrude . . ."

"Hey, Joe!" shouted a voice from behind them. "Wait up!"

Derek Hannon appeared at the door of the police station. He was carrying his sopping Wizards and Warriors outfit in a plastic bag and was wearing a pair of pants about two sizes too short for his long legs.

"I wanted to talk to you before you got away, Joe," Derek said. "I just wanted to apologize again for some of the things I said and did back in the dungeon. You're an all-right guy, Joe. Listen, I've got tickets for the big game this weekend in New York City. I was going to take this girl I know, but I was wondering if you'd like to come along instead."

"Sure!" said Joe. "I'd love it. I haven't been to a game in New York for years."

"Uh, you wouldn't have a third ticket for that game, would you?" asked Frank wistfully.

"Sorry, Frank. Only two. Maybe next time . . ."

"Hold on, guys," said Chet Morton, pushing his way awkwardly through the front door of the police station with his arms stuffed full of food. "I need a lift."

"Uh, okay, Chet," said Frank. "Where'd you get all the food?"

"Vending machines," he said. "Let's see, I've got three sandwiches, a couple of colas, four candy bars . . ."

"You must be on a diet," said Joe.

"It'll keep me until I get home," said Chet.

"It's a good thing that bag of snacks was still in the van," said Joe, "or Chet would have eaten the upholstery on the way over here."

"So," Frank asked Chet, "think you've had enough of Wizards and Warriors for a while?"

"Yeah, I think so," said Chet. "It was kind of a boring game, anyway. And I had this great idea while we were in the dungeon."

"Really?" asked Joe. "What was it?"

"Well, there's a hobby I've always wanted to try. It's called spelunking—cave exploring. There's this new cave that was just discovered outside of Bayport and I wondered if you guys would like to help me explore . . . Hey! Let go of my collar, Joe! You're going to make me drop the food!"

"Maybe if we take him back into the station, they'll lock him up for his own good," said Joe, dragging Chet toward the door.

"Nah," said Frank. "They couldn't afford to feed him. I guess we're stuck with him."

149

"Aw, come on, you guys," Chet protested. "It was just an idea."

"Eat your food, Chet, and keep your ideas to yourself," suggested Joe.

"Now *that's* a good idea!" said Chet, popping half a sandwich into his mouth as he smiled broadly.

THE HARDY BOYS® SERIES By Franklin W. Dixon

NANCY DREW® MYSTERY STORIES By Carolyn Keene

- ☐ THE TRIPLE HOAX—#57
  69153 $3.50
- ☐ THE FLYING SAUCER MYSTERY—#58
  72320 $3.50
- ☐ THE SECRET IN THE OLD LACE—#59
  69067 $3.50
- ☐ THE GREEK SYMBOL MYSTERY—#60
  67457 $3.50
- ☐ THE SWAMI'S RING—#61
  62467 $3.50
- ☐ THE KACHINA DOLL MYSTERY—#62
  67220 $3.50
- ☐ THE TWIN DILEMMA—#63
  67301 $3.50
- ☐ CAPTIVE WITNESS—#64
  70471 $3.50
- ☐ MYSTERY OF THE WINGED LION—#65
  62681 $3.50
- ☐ RACE AGAINST TIME—#66
  69485 $3.50
- ☐ THE SINISTER OMEN—#67
  62471 $3.50
- ☐ THE ELUSIVE HEIRESS—#68
  62478 $3.50
- ☐ CLUE IN THE ANCIENT DISGUISE—#69
  64279 $3.50
- ☐ THE BROKEN ANCHOR—#70
  62481 $3.50
- ☐ THE SILVER COBWEB—#71
  70992 $3.50
- ☐ THE HAUNTED CAROUSEL—#72
  66227 $3.50
- ☐ ENEMY MATCH—#73
  64283 $3.50
- ☐ MYSTERIOUS IMAGE—#74
  69401 $3.50
- ☐ THE EMERALD-EYED CAT MYSTERY—#75
  64282 $3.50
- ☐ THE ESKIMO'S SECRET—#76
  62468 $3.50
- ☐ THE BLUEBEARD ROOM—#77
  66857 $3.50
- ☐ THE PHANTOM OF VENICE—#78
  66230 $3.50

- ☐ THE DOUBLE HORROR
  OF FENLEY PLACE—#79
  64387 $3.50
- ☐ THE CASE OF
  THE DISAPPEARING DIAMONDS—#80
  64896 $3.50
- ☐ MARDI GRAS MYSTERY—#81
  64961 $3.50
- ☐ THE CLUE IN THE CAMERA—#82
  64962 $3.50
- ☐ THE CASE OF THE VANISHING VEIL—#83
  63413 $3.50
- ☐ THE JOKER'S REVENGE—#84
  63414 $3.50
- ☐ THE SECRET OF SHADY GLEN—#85
  63416 $3.50
- ☐ THE MYSTERY OF MISTY CANYON—#86
  63417 $3.50
- ☐ THE CASE OF THE RISING STARS—#87
  66312 $3.50
- ☐ THE SEARCH FOR CINDY AUSTIN—#88
  66313 $3.50
- ☐ THE CASE OF
  THE DISAPPEARING DEEJAY—#89
  66314 $3.50
- ☐ THE PUZZLE AT PINEVIEW SCHOOL—#90
  66315 $3.95
- ☐ THE GIRL WHO COULDN'T REMEMBER—#91
  66316 $3.50
- ☐ THE GHOST OF CRAVEN COVE—#92
  66317 $3.50
- ☐ THE CASE OF
  THE SAFECRACKER'S SECRET—#93
  66318 $3.50
- ☐ THE PICTURE PERFECT MYSTERY—#94
  66315 $3.50
- ☐ THE SILENT SUSPECT—#95
  69280 $3.50
- ☐ THE CASE OF THE PHOTO FINISH—#96
  69281 $3.50
- ☐ THE MYSTERY AT
  MAGNOLIA MANSION—#97
  69282 $3.50
- ☐ NANCY DREW® GHOST STORIES—#1
  69132 $3.50

and don't forget...THE HARDY BOYS® Now available in paperback

Simon & Schuster, Mail Order Dept. ND5
200 Old Tappan Road, Old Tappan, NJ 07675
Please send me copies of the books checked. Please add appropriate local sales tax.

☐ Enclosed full amount per copy with this coupon
(Send check or money order only.)
Please be sure to include proper postage and handling:
95¢—first copy
50¢—each additonal copy ordered.

☐ If order is for $10.00 or more,
you may charge to one of the
following accounts:
☐ Mastercard   ☐ Visa

Name _____ Credit Card No. _____

Address _____

City _____ Card Expiration Date _____

State _____ Zip _____ Signature _____

Books listed are also available at your local bookstore. Prices are subject to change without notice.   NDD-30